# Her eyes reflected her inner loneliness

"What do you do," Maggie pleaded, "when there's a need in you and the one person who might fulfill it turns away?"

Ian's control slipped and naked yearning flickered in the black depths of his eyes. Then with a shuddering expulsion of breath he gathered her in his arms and his mouth was on hers. It was a kiss so draining in its impact that her need became his. Their bodies strained closer.

Then suddenly Ian wrenched his mouth away, shaking his head in urgent denial. "I don't want you, Maggie...we'd devour each other."

"Maybe I want to be devoured," Maggie said slowly.

"Well I don't." His words were spoken with deadly emphasis. "I've fought too hard to carve out my own identity."

# Books by Emma Darcy

These books may be available at your local bookseller.

For a free catalog listing all titles currently available,
send your name and address to:

Harlequin Reader Service
P.O. Box 52040, Phoenix, AZ 85072-2040
Canadian address: Stratford, Ontario N5A 6W2

# EMMA DARCY

## tangle of torment

**Harlequin Books**

TORONTO • NEW YORK • LONDON
AMSTERDAM • PARIS • SYDNEY • HAMBURG
STOCKHOLM • ATHENS • TOKYO • MILAN

Harlequin Presents first edition April 1984
ISBN 0-373-10680-7

Original hardcover edition published in 1983
by Mills & Boon Limited

# CHAPTER ONE

THE elevator doors opened and the smile on Maggie's face lost its vibrancy. She stepped out automatically, her gaze sweeping around in disbelief, a sharp sense of claustrophobia stifling her breath. The whole floor had been partitioned into little cubicles and the only desk in sight was the floor receptionist's. From out of the maze of woodwork stepped Rhonda Farley. She caught sight of Maggie and grinned at her stunned expression.

'Ghastly, isn't it?'

'I was beginning to wonder if I'd got out on the wrong floor. Who perpetrated this horror?'

'Ssh!' Rhonda warned. 'These days you can't tell who's listening. The new boss, Ian Drake, has arrived with a vengeance! How are you, Maggie? You look well enough.'

Maggie hitched herself on to Rhonda's desk as the receptionist settled into her chair. She had felt very well up until a few moments ago; now her hands fluttered in a gesture of uncertainty. 'I'm fine. I still get the occasional dizzy spell, but not enough to worry me. Dan didn't want me to come back to work for another week, but I think he was arguing from a personal viewpoint.'

She glanced down at the beautiful sapphire and diamond ring on her finger and sighed. The fact that her fiancé was also a doctor inclined him to be over-protective. He had not liked her stubbornness and had only reluctantly given in to her decision to return to work. Maggie had been fed up with being a pampered patient. A month without the stimulus of the work she enjoyed had made her irritable.

'You can't blame him,' Rhonda observed slyly. 'Much nicer for him to have you on hand all the time instead of only at weekends. Besides, you should be careful. Pneumonia's not something you throw off quickly.'

'Don't you start on me!' Maggie retorted in mock exasperation. 'Mum and Dan gave me more than enough argument, thank you very much. Anyhow, to get back to immediate problems, I don't even know where my desk is in this . . . this mish-mash jungle.'

Rhonda laughed. 'You'll get used to it—we all had to. There's Peter getting out of the lift now. He'll be only too glad to show you around.' Her voice dropped to a whisper. 'He's been promoted, and does he love it!'

'Maggie! You're back at last!'

Peter Cameron advanced on her, his hands outstretched in welcome. He was a tall, slim, good-looking man who moved with the indolent grace of self-awareness. His fair hair had not one strand out of place from its fashionable cut, the light brown moustache was trimmed just so, and white even teeth flashed a winning smile. Impeccably dressed in a lightweight business suit, he conveyed the image of a successful executive, yet his attention to clothes was almost too fastidious. Maggie did not like him—slick, smarmy and too sexually orientated.

She slid off Rhonda's desk, preparing to palm

him off. Peter Cameron was all too eager with his hands as well as his eyes, which now ran over her. Maggie had worn a blue cotton-knit dress, splashed with large white indeterminate flowers. The fabric clung to her body and a white plaited belt accentuated her narrow waist. She knew that her curves drew attention from most males, but Peter's pale blue eyes lingered lasciviously on every one of them.

'Yes, I'm all here,' she said dryly. 'Now, maybe you can show me where to go and fill me in on what's been happening.'

'My pleasure,' he grinned wolfishly, taking her arm with elaborate courtesy. 'First let me tell you I have a new title.' The grin turned into a smirk as he noted her reaction. 'Yes, my dear Maggie, I am to all effects your most immediate boss, Floor Co-ordinator. I dish out the assignments and see that schedules are kept. I've been keeping the Jamieson account especially for your very individual talent. This is my office. Do come in while I get the file out for you.'

Maggie controlled a surge of resentment as she eyed the new executive desk, the comfortable leather chair and rows of sleek filing cabinets. Peter Cameron was certainly being done proud, and he was the last person Maggie wanted to have telling her what to do. Surprises were coming thick and fast this morning, and none of them pleasant.

He turned back to her with a large folder. She was familiar with the Jamieson file. It was one of the most lucrative accounts the Agency handled, and Maggie was accustomed to working on the large accounts. She had the individual flair which produced very effective advertising and had made quite a name for herself among people in the know. In fact the Maggie Tarrington name was successful enough for her to consider opening her own advertising agency, but her engagement to Dan Barlow had stopped her from thinking along those lines.

'Pretty classy, eh?' Peter said smugly, nodding to his office equipment.

'Useful,' was Maggie's terse comment. 'Now, where am I situated?'

'Ah, you're tucked away in a corner for complete privacy. Drake doesn't want any distractions from work.'

'Cutting off all communication, is he?' Maggie said levelly.

'Not at all. Cutting out the noise factor and the idle gossip.'

Maggie kept her reservations to herself. She had liked the open-plan floor where she could call across to anyone at any time. She was not at all sure she cared about being cut off from the easy camaraderie which had previously existed, but she could not really object to the cubicle she was shown into. It was well set up for her work, with a large desk and drawing board handily situated.

'There's a common room for morning tea and lunch where we can all get together,' Peter continued. 'It's been partitioned off near the exit to the wash-rooms. Everything's been set up with an eye to greater efficiency. I daresay Drake will want to have a few words with you this morning since you missed out on all the conferences.'

'Yes. I might even have a few words to say to Mr Drake myself,' Maggie said sweetly.

Peter eyed her with suspicion. 'A word of advice, Maggie—I'd watch that sharp tongue of yours if I were you. I don't think feminine charms, even yours, would affect his judgment one iota.'

'Thank you, Peter. It may surprise you to know I've never traded on feminine charms as far as work is concerned, and I don't expect men to hold my femininity against me. Now, I'd like to get my new bearings alone, if you don't mind.'

He eyed her shapely legs as she sat down and crossed them. Maggie automatically twitched her skirt down.

'On the other hand, I bet a girl like you doesn't walk into his office every day.' He grinned and made his exit before Maggie could think of a stinging retort.

She sighed and settled back in her chair. It was not that she disliked compliments, but sometimes she wished her physical attributes were not such a distraction from her as a person. She didn't wish herself to be any different. That would be stupid, and Maggie was far from stupid. She liked her face, the smooth, clean lines of her features, nothing irregular, everything well-shaped. She even liked her neutral grey eyes because eye-shdaow gave her the versatility to wear any colour successfully. Her hair was her most attractive feature, a raven-black mass of waves, curling down to just above her shoulders. It was a stunning contrast to her pale skin, and the effect was highlighted by thick eyelashes and the sharp black arch of her brows.

No one in her right mind would object to having the favours she was blessed with, but sometimes Maggie wondered if even Dan saw beneath the surface to any depth. She glanced down at the ring on her finger. I'm twenty-five years old and if I don't marry Dan, who will I ever marry? she thought despondently. He was intelligent, good-looking, athletic, amusing company. What more did she want in a man? It was crazy to entertain any doubts. Her mother was enraptured with Dan as a prospective son-in-law. No one could be more eligible in Fay Tarrington's eyes. His charm and confidence made him a popular doctor. His natural ability made him a good doctor. There was no obvious fault in him, and as her mother said, if Maggie waited much longer for a husband, she would be too old to have children.

She shrugged off her thoughts. This was not the time or the place to mull over the wisdom of marrying Dan Barlow. It was Peter Cameron's promotion which needed thinking about. Maggie ground her teeth in fierce resentment. There had been quite a flutter around the office just before she was struck down with pneumonia. Ian Drake's imminent takeover of the executive position was rumoured to be the beginning of sweeping changes. Maggie had not been perturbed, secure in the sure knowledge of her talent, but to come back and find Peter Cameron placed in a supervisory position over her was galling indeed.

She sourly admitted that Peter was good at organising other people into work. He cleverly disguised his own minor ability by using the talented human resources around him. The man was a poser, standing on the shoulders of more able workers, and he would have undoubtedly received a hefty rise in salary with the new title.

That stung Maggie even more. She glared at the Jamieson file. Why was she being handed the responsibility of the most important accounts when Peter Cameron was collecting titles and more money? Anger began a slow burn. So Ian Drake was going to see her this morning, was he? She was tempted to throw the Jamieson file on his desk and tell him to get Peter Cameron to handle it.

There was a knock on her door and she glanced around to see Rhonda's cheeky grin.

'Just as well it's me and not the boss-man himself! You're mooning, Maggie. Better brighten up. Mr Drake wants you up in his office.'

The two girls liked one another, which was just as well, because they were the only two females on this floor. Rhonda was always bemoaning her freckled skin and ginger hair, but she was really very pretty, her gamin face enlivened by a bright, friendly personality and the wide green eyes which were now twinkling at Maggie.

'What's he like, Rhonda?'

'Smashing, in a cool, remote way. Pity he's taken. He's engaged to be married, worse luck, and he must be a one-woman man. He barely looks at me. I might as well be office furniture. Maybe you'll rate a once-over.'

'Who cares?' Maggie shrugged as she prepared to follow Rhonda along the newly constructed corridor.

'It's all right for you—you've got your man. Here am I still hunting.' She sighed and pulled a wry face. 'Maybe some day I'll get lucky. Better hurry now, Maggie. He's in Becker's old office.'

Maggie did not bother waiting for the elevator. The executive office was only one flight up, so she took the stairs. It was a mistake. Halfway up her head started whirling and when she reached the top she had to stand still to steady herself. It irritated her that her balance was still affected. It was a month now since she had been hospitalised with pneumonia and she had only been seriously ill for a few days. The rest of the time had been spent convalescing, and still she was not right.

She drew in a deep breath and opened the door into the executive suite. Jane Carfield favoured her with a cold look. No change had been made here. Ian Drake had obviously inherited Becker's old secretary. She was a waspish spinster of middle age, super-efficient but not a person to welcome anyone with open arms. The way she looked down her long nose, tightened her thin lips, patted her bun and adjusted her glasses always made Maggie expect a sniff of annoyance at the inconsiderate interruption to work.

'Go right in. Mr Drake's expecting you,' she said without the grace of a greeting.

Maggie threw her a bright smile in the vain hope of shaming her, then gave a courtesy knock on Ian Drake's door and went in. Ian Drake rose to his feet immediately. He was not a tall man, not much above medium height, but if his tailor was not sewing deception he was powerfully built. He projected power as he rounded the desk and held out a strong hand.

'Miss Tarrington,' he murmured politely, his voice soft but far from weak. The deep timbre of it was modulated to produce a suggestion of intimate interest. 'I hope you're completely recovered.'

'Yes, thank you,' she replied crisply.

He barely touched her hand before gesturing to a chair. 'Please sit down. There are several matters for discussion.'

She studied his face as he resumed his position behind the large executive desk. It was very much a poker face, she decided, handsome in an angular way but devoid of any telltale expression. His hair was dark brown with no grey apparent, even though he looked to be in his mid-thirties. His eyes were almost black, sharp, piercing eyes, more so because they were deeply set below very definite, straight brows. The slightly hawkish nose was balanced by a square jawline. The only softness in his face was his mouth, which was perfectly shaped and more full-lipped than was usual in a man. He looked at her appraisingly but with no hint of sexual interest.

'You seem rather pale, Miss Tarrington. I hope you haven't hurried back here before you should. The after-effects of pneumonia are not to be disregarded,' he said with slow deliberation.

'I'm naturally pale, Mr Drake,' she answered levelly. 'I wouldn't have returned if I felt I couldn't cope.'

A slight wave of his hand dismissed the matter of her health. 'Well, as you can see, we've made a few changes here in your absence. I hope you find your new office satisfactory?'

'I may get used to it. You surely don't expect an informed opinion from half an hour's acquaintance with it.'

Her tart reply sharpened his eyes and one eyebrow rose fractionally as he reconsidered her. Maggie stared back unwaveringly, still simmering with resentment over Peter Cameron's promotion.

'I think you have something you wish to say, Miss Tarrington.'

'I'll listen first, Mr Drake.'

'You don't like the new office set-up?'

'It probably has its merits. First impressions are not necessarily correct ones.'

He nodded, picked up a pencil from his desk and balanced it between his two index fingers as he leaned back in his chair. 'You don't like Cameron's promotion.'

Anger mixed with annoyance at his accurate perception. Maggie forced back a hot-blooded retort. It would do no good to lose her temper in front of this man. She substituted cautious words for the impulsive ones which had leapt to her tongue. 'No doubt you have some cogent reason for promoting him over my head. I'd like to hear it.'

His lips curved slightly in appreciation of her control. 'You think the promotion should have been yours.'

'My record speaks for itself, Mr Drake. I presume you've gone through the personnel files before making your decision.'

He nodded.

'This morning I was handed the Jamieson account. That's quite a responsibility, Mr Drake,' she added pointedly.

'One I'm sure you will handle in your usual brilliant fashion, Miss Tarrington. I'm fully aware of your capabilities. The report on you from the industrial psychologist was very informative. "Margaret Tarrington has the ability to do almost anything she wishes, a natural facility for mathematics and words, organisational talent and wide, creative powers." You are top of the staff in every capacity tested. A person of your talent and intelligence cannot be overlooked, Miss Tarrington, but a person of your staying power is another consideration altogether. I understand you are engaged to be married.'

Maggie sucked in her breath but could not quench the fire which exploded in her brain. 'So,' she hissed, 'I should have known! I hear that you're also engaged to be married, Mr Drake. It hasn't stopped you taking up a position of power.'

'Is power what you want, Miss Tarrington?' he asked coldly. 'Which do you enjoy the most, organising or creating? I would have thought organisation of material was hack-work compared to creating something new.'

Maggie did not answer. She was fighting for control.

'Would you really like to see Cameron doing the Jamieson account while you spend your time hassling people on the administrative side?'

No! her brain screamed emphatically, despite her emotional reaction. 'I will not stand for Peter Cameron hassling me in any shape or form,' she said tightly. 'If you think for one moment I will tolerate that peewit brain telling me what to do, you can think again, Mr Drake!'

His mouth curved sardonically. 'Strong words, Miss Tarrington, and a little harsh, I think.

Cameron does have organisational ability. No creativity, perhaps. But he's the man for the job and he'll be here long after you resign.'

'Maybe that resignation you so blithely presume will be in the pipeline before even you expect it, Mr Drake, and along with it might go some of your more important accounts. I wonder if you considered that as well as my forthcoming marriage,' she replied acidly.

His expression tightened, becoming even more impenetrable at her implied threat. His eyes bore into hers, hard coals of darkness, revealing nothing. 'Yes, I considered it. That's why I called you up here. You're a valuable asset to this agency and your salary did not reflect your value. Name your price, Miss Tarrington. I have no wish to lose you, but I will not promote you out of an area where you excel.'

Although she was reluctant to admit it, he was right. She would hate Peter's new job. She preferred to work on her own. Explaining things to other people frustrated her, particularly when they did not share her vision of what should be. 'What's Peter Cameron's salary?' she asked abruptly.

'I'm sure you realise that's confidential.'

'I want whatever he's getting plus a bonus for every account I handle, the bonus to reflect the satisfaction of the customer.'

'Agreed,' he nodded.

'And I don't want Peter bugging me,' she insisted.

'Anything else? Perhaps you'd like a new title?' he asked dryly.

'I don't need ego-trips, Mr Drake, just fair

play. I've considered opening my own agency. It doesn't suit me at the moment. It may never suit me, but don't underestimate me. I'm good and I know I'm good.'

'Yes, I'm sure you do,' he replied softly, and Maggie felt she had been subtly slapped down for her arrogance. 'Do we have everything settled to your satisfaction now?'

Her aggression wilted. She paused to take stock and then nodded.

'Good. Cameron can save you time if you're prepared to use him. You should realise that.'

'Perhaps, Mr Drake, but the help he can give me carries an irritating price,' said Maggie with an acid little smile.

'You've lost me, I'm afraid.'

'Let's just say I'd accept his help more readily if I were a man.'

The dark eyebrows drew together in one beetling line and he lobbed the pencil he had been playing with back on the desk before leaning forward. His eyes skated over her once again and Maggie flushed at the cold, sexual appraisal.

'I see,' he murmured, hooding his eyes so that Maggie could not form an opinion as to what he saw. 'I would not have thought that type of attention would bother you, however . . .'

'I wonder how long you'd keep a secretary who kept referring to your physique every time she handed you some papers, who tried to touch you at every opportunity. Maybe you wouldn't find it at all irritating, Mr Drake, but I do,' Maggie snapped.

He gave a light shrug. 'Do you want me to have a word with him?'

'No. I'm simply explaining why I prefer to do things in my own way, without Peter breathing down my neck or assuming a position of authority over me. I'll organise my own work.'

'Very well, I think we understand each other. Play it any way you like, Miss Tarrington, so long as you keep delivering what our customers want.'

He stood up, prepared to show her out of the office. Without thinking Maggie rose too quickly and the sudden movement rocked her equilibrium. The blood drained from her face and she swayed. A strong hand clutched her shoulder, steadying her, and she gradually focussed on eyes full of dark concern.

'All right?' he murmured.

'Yes. I'm sorry, that was stupid of me. I have to go slowly,' she mumbled, feeling oddly agitated by his nearness.

'You haven't fully recovered,' he stated with a quick frown. 'Why did you return too soon?'

She forced a wry smile. 'I'm fit enough to work, Mr Drake, and I couldn't stand another week of idleness.'

He returned her smile and suddenly his face had an immense charm. 'The symptom of a workaholic, Miss Tarrington. I can well appreciate your frustration, but do go slowly. We can't afford a relapse. The Jamieson account awaits your touch.'

Maggie had the oddest sense of recognition, as if a direct link was formed between them, one mind seeing a kinship in the other. She saw his eyes flicker with rejection and his hand was abruptly withdrawn from her shoulder. A convulsive shiver ran over her skin. When he opened his office door for her, she passed by him quickly with barely a nod of acknowledgement.

She tried to order her thoughts while she waited for the elevator, but they were a blur of confusion. It was not until she was reseated at her own desk that she could revise the whole interview clearly. Ian Drake was a very smart man, she decided somewhat ruefully. He had drawn her out, giving nothing away himself until he had pinpointed precisely what she wanted. Then without moving a millimetre from his own position he had resolved the problems she had presented quickly and effectively. Yes, he was a very smart man, and Maggie had very mixed feelings about him. Her initial antagonism had given way to a grudging respect and something else from which she shied. Deliberately she opened the Jamieson file and immersed herself in work.

The toy company had come up with an original concept, a new range of games and toys related to a science-fictional planet called Tigaworld. The idea was to persuade families into acquiring everything offered. For pre-schoolers there was Tigaveld, a fuzzy-felt creation of a whole world of fantastic flora and fauna, space vehicles and glamorous buildings, and the Tigazens them-selves, beautiful cat-people. TigaTess and TigaTim were dolls to be costumed in glittering splendour. TigAttack was a board and dice game requiring strategic skill as well as luck. The top-drawer of the range was a sophisticated electronic game, TigaBlitz, a deadly space-war where the wrong move meant annihilation.

Excitement stirred in Maggie's blood. She liked the concept. It fired her imagination, demanding an advertising campaign which would be compelling in its impact on the public. This Christmas the toy market would be dominated by Tigaworld, if she could produce the right idea. Tomorrow she would go to Jamieson's factory, see all the toys, play with them, immerse herself in Tigaworld. Something would eventually click into her mind. It always did, sharp, compelling and beautifully exciting.

'Hey, snap out of it, Maggie! You missed morning tea and now it's lunchtime. Come and share my diet biscuits.'

Maggie started out of her concentration and glanced around at Rhonda.

'You really are the limit,' her friend chided. 'I swear you go off into a world of your own when you get your teeth into something. Do come on— I'm dying to hear what you thought of Ian Drake!'

'Okay,' Maggie smiled.

She picked up the bag of fruit she had brought for lunch and accompanied Rhonda to the common room. Some of the men were setting up a game of cards and they greeted her cheerily, wisecracking about her health. She retorted in kind and they all laughed and declared it was good to see her back. Rhonda operated the new coffeematic machine which had been installed and nodded to the armchairs in a corner. The card game started and the two girls relaxed together.

'Well?' Rhonda said archly.

Maggie shrugged. 'What do you want me to

say? Yes, he's attractive, very cool, very competent and a top executive if I'm any judge.'

Rhonda sighed. 'I think he's a real dish. He sends tingles up my spine every time those sexy eyes look at me.'

'Sexy?' Maggie gave a rippling laugh. 'That's about the last way I'd describe them!'

'Oh, I don't mean like Peter,' Rhonda put in hurriedly. 'I mean they seem to know everything, as if he can take one look at you and nothing's hidden from him. It's almost frightening in a delicious kind of way. Brrr!' She gave an expressive shiver and Maggie almost choked on a piece of apple. 'I suppose you're immune what with Dan and all,' Rhonda continued blithely, 'but I love men who sort of exude that kind of power, like that actor, you know, who played the main part in *The Power Game*. He might have been short, but boy, oh, boy, was he sexy! You can grin at me, Maggie Tarrington, but Ian Drake's got it as far as I'm concerned. I do wish he wasn't taken.'

'How do you know he is?' Maggie asked curiously.

'He left word at the telephonist's desk that his fiancée, Patricia Hollis, was to be put through to him at any time. Linda says she sounds nice, not that she listened in, but you know, when she asks to be connected. Apparently she's a hairdresser.'

'A hairdresser?' Maggie frowned. 'Surely not.'

'Why not? Linda says it's a hairdressing salon that answers when Ian Drake calls her.'

'Oh well, that sounds conclusive.'

'Why were you surprised?'

Maggie shrugged. 'I don't know. Somehow it didn't seem to fit. He's so ... oh, I don't know.'

Rhonda wrinkled her pert nose. 'Mmm, I know what you mean, but maybe he likes to relax away from work with someone a bit more lightweight. I bet she's blonde and soft and cuddly, the direct opposite of him. They say opposites attract.'

'Yes, I guess so,' Maggie agreed, repressing an odd feeling of disappointment. It was none of her business whom Ian Drake found attractive and she should not care. She deftly turned the conversation towards Rhonda's social life and was amused by a stream of lively comments.

'Anyhow, that's enough of me,' Rhonda declared with a sigh. 'What about you and Dan? Have you set your marriage date yet?'

'Yes—February the tenth. That gives us four months to get ourselves organised. I don't know where we're going to live. It's a long way to commute from Wallareen each day, but he's finally accepted that I like to work.'

'You're mad, Maggie,' Rhonda announced with a shake of her head. 'Why don't you put your feet up and let him support you if that's what he wants to do? Besides, you'll start having babies soon enough.'

'Will I?'

'Of course you will. Don't be dopey. You're twenty-five, no sense in wasting time if you want a family.'

'No, I expect you're right,' Maggie sighed, but a nameless fear clutched at her heart, gnawing at her even when she returned to her desk after the lunch-hour.

It was stupid to feel frightened, she reasoned angrily. It was every woman's dream to get

married and have a family. Dan would be a good
husband and father. She had made up her mind,
given him her word, and yet . . .

Stop it, you fool of a woman, she told herself
sternly. Rhonda was right. Her mother was right.
She felt more for Dan than she had ever felt for
any other man and she would be content with
him and the life he offered her. She fixed her
attention on the Jamieson file and determinedly
blocked her mind to anything else.

# CHAPTER TWO

'WELL, I'm glad you feel happy now, darling, but he was right, you know. There was no point in promoting you,' Dan commented, an indulgent tone in his voice.

Maggie automatically bristled. 'What if it was a position I wanted and deserved?'

He sighed.

She knew it was trying his patience, but some devil inside her was whipping her on. 'Why should I be denied promotion just because I'm getting married?'

'Maggie, don't make a fight of it, love.' He leaned over from the driver's seat and lightly caressed her cheek, his soft brown eyes telling her how much she was wanted. 'Let it go. It doesn't matter.'

He kissed her and Maggie let it go, allowing all her tormenting doubts to be swamped by the surge of sensuality Dan so expertly aroused.

'This is all that matters,' he whispered huskily against her lips. 'Love me, darling.'

Maggie responded recklessly. A tight coil of inner desperation demanded to be blotted out, and passion presented an all too easy means. Dan was no immature, inexperienced lover. He savoured every liberty she allowed him, intent on giving pleasure as well as taking it. She made no protest when he unbuttoned her blouse and slid his hand over the fullness of her breats, nor when he pushed her flimsy bra aside for more intimate contact.

'You're so beautiful,' he murmured as he glanced down at the exposed peaks.

He bent to kiss them, to play erotic games with his tongue, and Maggie's senses swam with waves of pleasure. Her fingers thrust agitatedly through his hair, entwining themselves in the dark-blond curls. Her breath came in excited gasps and when he took her mouth again she was lost, reeling down a deep well of desire. Then suddenly the onslaught of sensuality ceased. Dan pulled the edges of her blouse roughly together, gave her a long, searing look and gunned the powerful Jaguar motor.

'Where are you going?' Maggie asked in bewilderment, looking back at her mother's home.

'To my apartment. I'm not making love to you in a car, Maggie.'

His words hit her like a wet cloth, dampening the heat which had been generated. In a flash of self-honesty Maggie knew she would have let him possess her a few moments ago. He had every right to think she was ready to be his. They were going to be married. There was no arguable reason for resisting that final intimacy—and yet panic fluttered along her veins.

'No, Dan, please. Take me back home,' she said urgently.

He flashed her an incredulous look. 'You've got to be joking!'

Shame burnt across her cheeks. Her abandoned response to his lovemaking was coming home to roost. 'I'm sorry, Dan. Please go back. I don't want to . . . to go to your apartment.'

He angrily pulled the car over to the kerb and thumped the driving wheel in frustration. 'Why, for God's sake! What is it with you, Maggie? You drive me out of my mind and then you switch off. Haven't we made a commitment to each other? I love you. What more do you want?'

'I don't know.' Tears brimmed up in her eyes and she shook her head helplessly. 'I don't know, Dan. All I know is I'm not ready for that.'

'Do you think you'll make it by our wedding night?' he demanded bitterly. 'Damn it, Maggie! You wanted me as much as I wanted you back there.' He grabbed her roughly by the shoulders, his fingers digging into the soft flesh as he shook her. 'What is it? You're sure as hell not frigid!' He saw the tears in her eyes and groaned, pulling her into his arms with quiet desperation. 'Oh, Maggie, Maggie! What am I going to do with you?'

'Just hold me, Dan, hold me tight,' she whispered, clinging to him. 'Make me feel safe.'

'What are you frightened of, love?' he asked gently, soothing her with his warm embrace.

'I think I'm frightened of change. I don't know if I can cope with being a suburban housewife. I don't think I even have any maternal instincts. What if I'm a bad mother, Dan? What if I can't cope?'

'Darling, it's different with your own children, honestly!' He drew back and looked down at her anxious eyes, projecting a calm assurance. 'I've seen it dozens of times. You're not the only woman who's had those fears, but I can assure you that every baby I've delivered has been received with joy into its mother's arms. It'll be the same with you, believe me.' He smiled with soft tenderness. 'You'll have beautiful children, Maggie.'

'Oh, Dan!' she sighed. 'I'm such a fool. Why do you want to marry me?'

'Because I took one look at you and knew you had to be mine,' he answered complacently and then kissed her. 'Even if I do have to wait until our wedding night,' he added wryly as he let her go.

It was not the answer Maggie wanted. She sat in despondent silence, adjusting her clothing and doing up her buttons as he drove her back home. He escorted her to the front door and she had to force herself to relax and respond to his goodnight kiss.

'Let's have lunch at the Club before we play tennis tomorrow.'

'All right,' she agreed quickly. 'Pick me up at eleven-thirty.'

'Fine. I hope you have more peaceful dreams than I shall,' he said with a trace of his former frustration.

'I'm sorry, Dan,' she mumbled guiltily.

He tilted her chin up and brushed her lips with his. 'It's just as well I'm a patient man. Goodnight, my love.'

Maggie did not have peaceful dreams. She tossed and turned for much of the night, unable to settle her doubts. She worried that Dan did not really know her and then she worried that she did not really know him. She imagined them waking up one day to find they were strangers, each an alien to the other. She finally dropped into an exhausted sleep, having resolved nothing.

All during their tennis date the next day, Maggie tried to look at Dan objectively. His white shorts and T-shirt revealed his splendid physique and highlighted the depth of his tan. The bright sunlight burnished the dark gold of his hair and made the light down glisten on his muscular arms and legs. His clean-cut features were, if anything, too handsome, and he walked with the confidence of a man who knew he drew admiration.

He drew people to him too. Over lunch they were joined by several other couples. Dan was witty and charming. The conversation was lively. His manners had that easy polish which comes with confident maturity. He was successful, popular and well-respected.

Later, as they played a few hard sets of tennis, she watched the smooth grace which came with perfect co-ordination. He was a natural athlete and his body proclaimed the fact. Maggie was a better than average tennis player and he matched his game to hers, generous in sportsmanship. There was very little to fault in Dan Barlow and Maggie knew other women envied her his attention.

The only thing that really irked her was his air of possessiveness, the pride he took in having her at his side, almost showing her off as a prize piece of property. He relished any look of envy directed at him and he displayed his ownership with frequent caresses. Maggie had the strangest feeling that she was playing a part, not really existing in the scene at all, that if she could divide herself from her body, her body would suffice for Dan's needs.

She felt disembodied for the rest of the weekend and was relieved to catch the train back into the inner city on Sunday night. At least the small apartment she leased had the merit of being hers alone. She did not have to cope with her mother's well-meant questions nor bear the weight of her mother's suffocating approval of Dan. She could be herself without having to smile or pretend or apologise for anything.

She felt a profound sense of satisfaction as she walked into her own living-room. It was cluttered with possessions. Dan had laughed when he first saw it, saying she must be a magpie, having collected such a vast assortment of things; books, records, cassettes, figurines, prints of her favourite paintings, souvenirs of her various holidays.

She looked with favour at the two large, comfortable armchairs. Her mother's home was all subdued elegance. Maggie had splashed out with a brilliant parrot and foliage cotton print which covered the loose-cushioned chairs and curtained the windows. It looked stunning against the deep red carpet. Dan should have said a parrot, she thought ironically, a bird of bright plumage. That's what he sees in me.

She made herself a cup of coffee and carried it over to the corner table. Ideas for Jamieson's new advertising campaign had been flitting through her mind and she wanted to jot them down and develop them. She pulled the cover off her typewriter and reached for some stationery. Other people might think she was mad to work in her leisure time, but she needed a diversion from

her personal problems anyhow. An overall plan
started evolving in her mind and by the time she
forced herself to go to bed she was too excited by
it to sleep well. She woke early and decided to go
into the office, and begin a proper layout.

The commuter rush had barely started and
there were empty seats on the bus. Usually it was
crowded by the time it reached her stop. Maggie
sat down and relaxed, reflecting on how much
she loved living in Paddington. It had the
atmosphere of something always happening. She
loved the city of Sydney with its heartbeat of
excitement. For weekends, Wallareen was pleasant, but she wondered if she would adjust to
living its more leisurely pace when she married
Dan.

Ten minutes later she was alighting near her
office building. The street had already begun to
hum with bustling people, but the lobby was all
air-conditioned quiet as she stepped inside. The
elevator doors were just starting to close.

'Wait!' she called out instinctively, and broke
into a run, her high heels clacking on the tiles as
she crossed the floor. She plunged through the
narrow opening, a smile on her lips. 'Thanks.'

One black eyebrow lifted. 'No trouble. You're
very early this morning, Miss Tarrington,' Ian
Drake commented, calmly pressing the button for
her floor.

'I couldn't sleep,' Maggie grinned, bubbling
over with enthusiasm. 'I've got the whole
Jamieson promotion in my head and I'm bursting
to put it down and look at it.'

His eyes glowed down at her with quick
appreciation. 'Compulsive, is it?'

'I can't help it.'

'I know.'

And in the same instant Maggie knew that he did know. Her smile faltered, her eyes questioning his in startled wonder.

He smiled. 'My expertise is in a different field, but once I attack a problem, the urge to get everything right is quite compulsive. Your floor, Miss Tarrington.'

The doors were sliding open. Maggie gave a quick, embarrassed nod and stepped out. She should not have gawked at him like an idiot, but it had felt so good to know that someone understood her inner elation. It had been a moment of sharing which she had never experienced before.

She wasted no time in organising the materials she wanted. The hours passed unnoticed as sketches, slogans, scenarios were filled out and perfected. Rhonda poked her head in at lunchtime, but Maggie waved her away. By the end of the day she was exhausted and exhilarated. She had it, precisely what was needed to launch the new range of toys on the market for Christmas. TV, radio, magazines; it was all there ready to take down to the Art Department for further polish. She went home and collapsed with fatigue.

The next morning she took a sheaf of papers down to Bert Oliver, confident that he would carry out her instructions. Bert was a clever artist, capable of projecting the light touch of humour in his drawings that she wanted. His own sense of humour tended to be rather off-beat, a deliberate defence for his unconventional lifestyle. Maggie liked him and she liked working with him. He was perceptive and sensitive to her feelings and she rather enjoyed his bitchy comments on life in general. He was nodding over her explanations, patting his prematurely bald head in heavy concentration, when Peter Cameron interrupted them.

'What are you doing down here, Maggie?'

'What does it look as if I'm doing?' she retorted impatiently.

'Inter-department work is channelled through me, or didn't you know?' he said with pronounced pique.

She was tempted to tell him to get lost, but tact prevailed. 'I only answer to Mr Drake, Peter. Didn't he make that clear to you? Maybe you should have a word with him.'

'I'll do that,' he said curtly, and left them alone.

'Naughty, naughty!' Bert grinned at her, his puckish face alive with glee.

'Oh, let's get on with it. I can't be bothered pandering to his ego.'

Bert would have obviously loved to dissect Peter's ego, but he saw the dismissal on Maggie's face and sighed. 'All right, little steamroller. Where do you want me to start?'

They worked together for the rest of the day as Maggie's vision took shape under Bert's flying pen.

'Okay, that's it. You've got it, Bert. I can leave it with you now,' she declared at last.

'Another winner, Maggie.'

She flushed with pleasure. 'Let's hope so.' Her eyes twinkled with private triumph. 'I've got a bonus riding on this one.'

'Do I get a share?'

She lauged at his comically hopeful look. 'You'll have to ask the boss.'

Exhilaration winged her feet upstairs where she came down to earth with an unpleasant bump. Peter Cameron was in her office cubicle looking over her notes.

'A slight invasion of privacy, Peter?' she asked coldly.

'It's very good, Maggie.'

'I don't recall asking you to give an opinion, let alone take a look.'

His eyes travelled over her speculatively. 'I bet Ian Drake took a look.'

The snide remark sent her temperature up several degrees, but she controlled her tongue. 'On the contrary, I've only taken Bert Oliver into my confidence. I prefer to display the polished product.'

'Oh, you're very polished, Maggie. You've even got Drake twisted around your finger,' he said derisively. 'Well, you might have been given total freedom between floors, but as a matter of professional courtesy, you could keep me informed of progress. I do have to liaise with clients, you know. We held the Jamieson account back for you and they're eager for a report.'

Maggie sighed and pushed her hair away from her forehead. 'I'm sorry, I didn't think. You didn't tell me it was urgent.'

'It's not really urgent,' he admitted reluctantly. 'But they are eager to see something.'

'I'll be ready for Friday if you want to set up a meeting—and Peter,' she added warningly, 'I don't like you poking around my desk. Don't do it again.'

'The prima donna speaks and I obey,' he said with a mocking gesture of obeisance.

'You may not like the arrangement, Peter, but I think you'd better agree to co-exist peaceably,' Maggie said tersely.

'Or you'll go running to Daddy Drake upstairs?'

'You just can't see it, can you?' she said cuttingly. 'You have to reduce everything to sex!'

'It's what makes the world go round.'

Her control slipped on his oily slickness. 'Not my world, buster. I like a straight line and I'll order my world my own way. Now you just hop on your merry-go-round and get the hell out of here.'

'Tut-tut! Language!'

'Out!' she pointed angrily.

He laughed, waving an admonishing finger which deliberately fell on her breast as he brushed past. She felt like yelling 'pervert!' after him, but restrained herself. He was simply an irritating pimple she had to live with and it was irrational to let him get under her whole skin.

Bert Oliver produced exactly what she wanted. The layouts were complete and ready for display by Thursday afternoon. Peter had informed her that the Jamieson executives were due to arrive in the screening room at ten o'clock on Friday morning. She arranged with Bert to set up the necessary equipment and felt satisfied that everything was under control.

Maggie dressed in what she privately called her professional clothes for the meeting. The white silk blouse had an elegant, floppy bow which offset the severity of the black gaberdine suit. She liked black and white, knew that it accentuated her colouring and yet was pleasingly discreet. Ian Drake was with Bert in the screening room when she arrived with her folder.

'Good morning,' she said, slightly surprised to find him there early.

He nodded. 'Everything appears to be in hand.' He glanced at his watch and then back to her. 'Do you need anything else for your demonstration, Miss Tarrington?'

'No. We're all organised. You can bring them in whenever they arrive, Mr Drake.'

His mouth curved into a slight smile. 'I'm quite looking forward to seeing the result of inspiration.'

'I hope you won't be disappointed,' she replied cautiously.

'I doubt it, Miss Tarrington. As you remarked before, your record speaks for itself. Besides, I must admit I've had a sneak preview from Oliver here. I'll see you both later.'

He made an abrupt exit, leaving Maggie with a bemused look on her face.

'Snap out of it, darling. He didn't even say you look stunning, which you do,' said Bert with a light smirk.

'I don't care. So long as he thinks my work's stunning. That's the whole point, dear Bert,' she replied blithely.

'No worry on that score. I think I've quite outdone myself.'

He struck a complacent pose and Maggie laughed. She felt more comfortable with Bert than any other man, probably because he was not the least bit interested in her body.

'He's very macho, though, isn't he?' he added slyly.

'Mr Drake?'

'The one and only.'

'I suppose he is.'

'Puts Dan in the shade?'

Maggie smiled, deflecting the barb. Bert took malicious pleasure in stirring up mischief between established couples, feeling out chinks in the relationship.

'Different type,' she declared carelessly. 'Come on, Bert, we've got work to do.'

'Slave-driver!'

The remark niggled at her mind as she went automatically about the preparations. Dan was superficially more attractive than Ian Drake. He was taller, his physique more in proportion. They had the same air of confidence, the same aura of success about them, and yet Maggie sensed a depth in Ian Drake which Dan seemed to lack.

At ten o'clock he returned with the Jamieson executives. Introductions were quickly dispensed and once the men were comfortably seated, Maggie signalled to Bert to begin. He switched off the lights and a joyous tingle of anticipation highlighted Maggie's confidence as silence fell expectantly.

The screen leapt into colourful life, dominated by a beautiful ginger tabby cat. Its immediate image was a contented domestic animal, lazily licking its paw. Then suddenly it looked up, straight into the viewer's eyes, and the sharp, threatening intelligence in the fierce yellow eyes warned that this was no ordinary cat. It stood, arched its back with haughty grace, gave a contemptuous flick of the tail, then stalked across a room to take up a commanding position behind a layout of Tigaworld. The film froze on that frame and Maggie began speaking.

'You have just met TigaTom. He will symbolise Tigaworld in every advertisement, lifting the ordinary to the extraordinary. His message is: take a second look, things are not what they seem. He throws out a challenge: I'm superior, I dare you to try this, compete if you can, my world dares you to enter.'

Vibrations of interest pervaded the room and Maggie's confidence leapt into overdrive as she instructed Bert to continue. Her voice sparkled with enthusiasm, expounding each new facet of the campaign while Bert illustrated her ideas on the screen. There was a spontaneous burst of applause when she finished. The lights were switched back on and her eyes went straight to Ian Drake. He smiled and she smiled back, intense gratification leaping between them.

She politely accepted the exuberant compliments heaped on her work, but no one else's opinion mattered so much as Ian Drake's. She glowed inside, happier than she had been for a long time. At his nod of approval she accepted the invitation to lunch with the Jamieson executives. They were eager to mull over the details of the campaign and she was only too pleased to assist them.

Maggie was riding on a high for the next two hours. At the restaurant Ian Drake sat back and watched her, only joining the conversation when

technical details needed more explanation. The
dark eyes glinted knowledge of her inner elation.
He knew how she felt and she knew he knew. It
was the most incredible sense of togetherness
Maggie had ever experienced. It was like
champagne in her blood, sparkling, heady, and
far more intoxicating than the wine they drank
with their meal.

The sensation was far too exhilarating to
question, nor did she question her heightened
anticipation when the Jamieson executives
departed and she was left alone with Ian Drake.
He summoned a taxi and handed her in. She
quickly moved over to give him seat-room, and
he settled beside her. As he leaned forward to
instruct the cab-driver his thigh pressed against
hers, and the physical awareness which ripped
through her had the jolt of an electric shock.
Maggie covered up by relaxing back against the
seat and closing her eyes.

'Tired?'

The deep voice held a soft intimacy which sent
a delicious shiver up her spine. She lifted her
lashes and smiled at him.

'Not really. I shouldn't ever drink wine with
lunch. I'm going to be perfectly useless all
afternoon.'

The black eyes twinkled with amusement.
'You'll be suffering anti-climax anyway. It's
terribly deflating to fade back down to mundane
matters.'

'You can read me like a book, can't you?'

He grinned. 'Some of the pages are familiar.
There's nothing more satisfying than when all the
pieces click together, the picture is complete and

you know for certain that your vision was right.'
His hands lifted in a careless gesture as he added
dryly, 'And it's pleasant when other people
acknowledge it.'

'Yes, it's pleasant,' she agreed on a sigh.

'But it doesn't count for much, does it? They
don't comprehend the obsessive drive for perfection which has created the end pattern, all the
irritations along the way, the frustration of trying
to explain to others what you want done.'

'Do you? Get frustrated, I mean,' she asked
curiously.

His smile had a tigerish quality. 'I have the
distinct advantage of holding the whip hand.
Theirs not to wonder why, theirs but to do or
die . . . or lose their jobs.'

Maggie laughed—then the amusement dancing
in their eyes suddenly changed. A vibrant
electricity charged the air between them, a
magnetic force which held them both captive.
The urge to draw together was almost compelling.
As Ian Drake's head inclined towards hers
Maggie's had lifted instinctively. Then he
abruptly cut the cord of attraction, turning away
from her and staring straight ahead. His hand
moved jerkily, removing the cigar which had
been thrust into his coat pocket by one of the
Jamieson men. His fingers fumbled with the
wrapping, then tore it off impatiently.

'Mind if I smoke?' he asked curtly without
looking at her.

'No, I don't mind,' she replied stiffly.

She had shrunk back in upon herself, her mind
in turmoil, appalled by the urgent desire which
had flared so spontaneously, heating her blood so

that even now a painful blush scorched her cheeks. She loved Dan. She was going to marry Dan, and there she had been, almost offering herself to another man, a man who was also emotionally committed to someone else. Guilt snaked a tortuous path around her heart, and before she could call back the words, they were blurting off her tongue in an oblique accusation.

'What's your fiancée like?' Immediately she tried to retract. 'I'm sorry, that was a very personal question. Please ignore it.'

She averted her head, staring blindly out of the side-window of the taxi, totally embarrassed. An awkward silence stretched between them, seeming to thicken the pungent cigar smoke. Maggie's throat felt constricted and she swallowed convulsively.

'Pat is, I think, the nicest woman I've ever met, a very giving person, very human in the best sense of the word.'

The words were slow and measured as if he was reminding himself of her quality. Maggie darted a glance at him, but his expression was shuttered. The eyes he turned on her gave nothing away. One black eyebrow rose fractionally.

'And your fiancé?'

Maggie was confused by a welter of emotions she could not begin to identify. 'Dan is . . . he's a gynaecologist.'

'That tells me he's intelligent and little else,' he prompted dryly.

'He's . . . he's just Dan,' she said limply, unable to add a catalogue of his qualities because suddenly they didn't seem enough.

'For a woman who deals in communication you're surprisingly sparse with your words of description, Miss Tarrington. Are you happy with him?'

'Yes, of course,' she answered quickly.

'Then that's all that matters. When are you getting married?'

'February. And you?'

'Not until April.'

The finality of those dates ended the conversation. Fortunately it was only a few minutes before the taxi pulled up outside their office building. Ian Drake helped Maggie out and would have retained a light hand on her elbow, but she moved away, finding the contact too disturbing. They walked across the lobby, consciously apart. An elevator was waiting at the ground floor, so there was only a moment's delay in pressing buttons.

'Take the afternoon off if you like,' he offered as the compartment purred upwards. 'You've earned it, and it'll give you an early start for the weekend.'

'Thank you,' Maggie replied, formally polite.

She was relieved when the elevator doors opened, giving her escape from the enforced confinement. Her physical awareness of Ian Drake had almost been suffocating. She strode quickly to the privacy of her own office cubicle. The Jamieson folder lay on her desk. Bert Oliver had obviously returned all her papers. She sank down in her chair, but the file remained closed. There was no way she could concentrate on work this afternoon. Ian Drake had perceived that only too well, and she had to wipe Ian Drake out of her mind.

Her hand reached for the telephone. She needed to see Dan, get herself straightened out. Fortunately the call was put through to him without delay.

'Dan, it's Maggie. I'm coming home early. Can you meet the five o'clock train?'

'Yes, but why the change? Are you sick, Maggie?' he asked in quick concern.

'No, I'm fine. I've been given an early mark for good work. I'll tell you all about it when I see you. Could we go out for dinner to celebrate?'

'My pleasure, darling. What are we celebrating?'

'I think we should celebrate you and me,' she said recklessly.

'Any time, my love, any time. In fact I can't wait. You've just ruined my concentration. My patients will probably suffer from negligence for the rest of the afternoon!'

'I love you, Dan,' she declared with a note of defiance he did not hear.

'That sounds even more promising! 'Bye for now.'

Maggie replaced the handset, picked up her handbag and walked out of the office, out of the building, determinedly leaving Ian Drake behind her, putting him at a distance both mentally and physically.

# CHAPTER THREE

MAGGIE alighted from the train and saw Dan bearing down on her, a beaming smile making his face more handsome than ever. He swept her into his arms and swung her around exuberantly.

'Ah! Don't tell me. Let me guess,' he said, holding her at arm's length and examining her from head to toe. 'You've got your professional clothes on. Therefore I deduce that the Jamieson mob went wild over your toy ads and you're a terribly clever girl.'

She laughed and gave him a quick kiss. 'Right in one!'

He tucked her under his arm possessively, picked up her suitcase and walked her to his car. 'And where would you like to go? I've booked tables at the Club, Roberto's and La Vie Parisienne, so you can have good old Australian, Italian or French food, whatever you wish, my lady fair.'

'Oh, French, most definitely.'

'I was hoping you'd feel like that,' he said with an exaggerated leer.

'You're incorrigible, Dan Barlow,' she teased him with her eyes.

'Only waiting to be encouraged, my love,' he retorted, and handed her into the car.

He drove her to her mother's home, stayed for a couple of drinks and then left to wash and change for their dinner date.

'You're positively glowing, Maggie,' her mother said with a warm note of approval. Her daughter's cheeks were lightly flushed and she did not see the feverish glitter in her eyes. 'I thought last weekend you still looked peaky. Are you over those dizzy spells?'

'Yes, Mum, no trouble. Are you playing Bridge tonight?'

'No. Dorothy's sick,' she sighed, obviously disappointed.

Maggie threw her a sympathetic look, knowing how much her mother's life revolved around her Bridge games. Maggie's father had died five years ago and Fay Tarrington had little else to interest her now. She had been left wealthy, with no need to work, and the social life she had led with her stockbroker husband had dwindled to a small circle of widows. She was still a very handsome woman, only fifty years of age, but she had shown no inclination to look for another husband. Maggie's parents had been very content together and Fay Tarrington's one obsession was to see her daughter happily married. Dan Barlow had been the answer to her prayers.

'I think I'll have a long bath and really give myself the glam treatment tonight,' Maggie announced with a smile.

'I'm sure Dan will appreciate it, dear. What are you going to wear?'

'The red crêpe, I think.' It was a rather daring little dress, almost backless and fitting snugly over her hips before flaring out. 'I feel like dancing.'

'Dan will love you in it,' her mother said indulgently.

'I hope he loves me anyhow,' Maggie tossed over her shoulder as she headed upstairs.

She sternly held back the creeping desperation which threatened her peace of mind. Having groomed herself to perfection she assessed the reflection in the mirror with almost grim satisfaction. The dress and the vibrant make-up had produced the desired effect. Her appearance was nearly a blatant sexual invitation. Tonight she wanted Dan's lovemaking. She wanted him to wipe out the image of Ian Drake, make her feel secure and happy, warmed by the love he had declared so fervently. She needed to test her own reactions, to choke off the worm of doubt which was writhing around her heart. The doorbell announced Dan's arrival. She splashed herself liberally with Arpège and went down to greet him.

The quickened gleam in Dan's eyes warned her that his anticipation of the night's pleasures had taken a gigantic leap forward. She fought down a tingle of apprehension and returned his smile. He made no effort to hide his desire as they drove to La Vie Parisienne. His gaze kept wandering to her, too hungry to concentrate on the road. Instead of feeling gratified Maggie felt uncertain and a little ashamed of her motives. All her inhibitions rose to mock her, but she determinedly pushed them aside, setting herself to be gay and amusing.

The dinner wine helped. She welcomed the alcoholic haze which made her feel pliant and mellow. She flirted outrageously with Dan, warming herself with the fire in his eyes, letting it encompass her. They danced and ate and drank and danced again.

'God, but you're beautiful!' Dan whispered, lightly stroking the bare skin of her back as they moved slowly around the pocket dance-floor. His lips brushed the hair away from her temples. 'I love you, particularly in this dress you're almost wearing, more especially if you were wearing nothing at all,' he added, a suggestive thickness in his voice.

'What if I were plain and ordinary? Would you love me then? What if I didn't have the figure to wear this dress?' she taunted provocatively.

His eyes gleamed wickedly. 'The question doesn't arise. You're you, quite, quite perfect, and I adore you.'

'Your prize possession,' she muttered on a defeated sigh.

His arms suddenly tightened around her. 'Let's get out of here.'

'No. I want to dance,' she pouted. 'I want to dance the night away.'

His hand thrust her more firmly against him, forcing an awareness of his needs. 'Baby doll, I can't wait much longer for you, patient man though I am. It's eating at me.'

Despite her resolve Maggie postponed the moment of sexual surrender. She was not yet ready. 'Let's sit down and have another drink.'

Her words were slurred and he glanced down at her more sharply. 'Don't you think you've had enough to drink?'

'Nope. I'm thirsty and I want to dance the night away. We'll have some more champagne to celebrate.'

She broke away from him and led the way back to their table. She knew she was behaving badly, stoking the fires of desire and then cooling them, but it was as if she was on a roller-coaster which was careering away with her, out of control. She almost fell into her chair and some of the champagne splashed on her hand as she tilted her glass in a toast.

'To us, Dan,' she murmured, and drained it without pausing for breath.

Dan frowned. 'What's got into you, Maggie?'

'I just want to be happy. I'm happy with you, Dan,' she declared with a glazed smile, determined on convincing herself. 'You love me, don't you?'

'You know I do.'

'And you want me to be happy.'

He nodded, eyeing her with some concern.

'Happy in my mind as well as my body,' she continued recklessly. 'Do you know what goes on in my mind, Dan? What goes tickety-tick-tick in my brain? Sometimes I get a lovely explosion of ideas, a beautiful pattern of interlocking pieces, and I'm totally obsessed with them. Everything else clicks off because there's no room for anything else. It's exciting and compelling, and I've got to channel it all out before I can pull the rest of me back together again. Do you understand that, Dan?'

'I'm not sure. What are you trying to say, Maggie?'

She sighed. 'If you don't know you don't know. He knows,' she added as a muttered afterthought.

'Beg pardon?'

She looked up and saw Dan as a stranger and she felt very cold. 'Fill my glass up again, please. I need to get warm.'

'I'll warm you, Maggie, if you'll only say yes.'

'All right, let's go,' she said decisively.

But she fell asleep as soon as the car was in motion and Dan took her home, half carrying her inside because her feet wouldn't walk properly.

'Sorry, Dan,' she mumbled as he tried to steady her.

'My fault. I should have called a halt before that last bottle of champagne. You're properly sozzled, love. Can you manage or will I take you up to bed?'

'I can manage. 'Night, Dan.'

He kissed her and her head reeled from the amount of alcohol she had consumed. Her response was limp and he let her go.

'See you tomorrow,' he murmured.

'Yes. Tomorrow. Tomorrow and tomorrow and tomorrow. That's how it'll be.'

He threw her an amused look as he opened the front door and then he was gone.

'That's how it'll be,' Maggie repeated wearily, 'and I don't know how I'll manage.' She started levering herself up the stairs, using the banister as a support. 'Why did you have to come into my life and complicate it, Ian Drake? I might have been happy. You're happy with your Pat. Why can't I be happy with my Dan?' She paused, frowning, and then continued hauling herself upwards. 'Damn you, Ian Drake! I'm going to be happy with Dan. He's good and kind and considerate and he loves me. Yes, he does. At least, I think he does. And he wants me. He definitely wants me.'

'Maggie!'

She looked up and saw her mother at the head of the stairs, her face lined with concern.

' 'Lo, Mum. I was just saying that Dan loves and wants me.'

'Of course he does, dear. What's the matter with you, clattering up the stairs and talking to yourself?'

'Had too much to drink. My fault.'

'Oh, Maggie! Come on, dear, I'll help you into bed.'

She allowed her mother to slide off her clothes and put her to bed, too listless to bother helping. Her mind kept racing around in circles, snatching at important things it couldn't quite grasp. She looked up at her mother's dear, familiar face, her eyes pleading for help.

'What am I going to do, Mum? Dan doesn't know me.'

'You're talking nonsense. Maggie. Best to go to sleep.'

She clutched at her mother's dressing-gown, insisting that she listen. 'No. Not like him. He knows me, Mum, but he doesn't want me, and I don't know what to do.'

'Maggie, you're confused. I don't know what you're talking about. Go to sleep, now, dear.'

'So confused . . . Don't go, Mum. I need you.'

Her mother sat on the edge of the bed and patted her shoulder comfortingly. 'We'll talk about it in the morning, Maggie. You go to sleep now and you'll feel better tomorrow.'

Tears started to her eyes and began trickling down her cheeks. 'Yes, all right, Mum. Tomorrow,' she whispered sadly. 'But there are so many tomorrows, and I don't know what to do.'

Her mother gave her a last reassuring pat and stood up to go. 'Sleep on it, dear.'

But sleeping solved nothing, and Maggie did not feel any better, not that day or the next. She found it impossible to communicate her emotional dilemma to either her mother or Dan. She was not even capable of putting it into words, let alone make them understand. The compelling affinity she had felt with Ian Drake plagued her thoughts all weekend.

Dan grew increasingly frustrated with what he saw as a retreat from her more promising behaviour of Friday night. They ended up quarrelling over her work. Somehow he had sensed that the seeds of her withdrawal lay there. They patched up their quarrel and Maggie returned to Paddington on Sunday night with even more relief than usual.

By mid-week she had convinced herself that her imagination had been over-active, exaggerating what had only been a combination of exhilaration over her success with the Jamieson account, and a sensitive appreciation of it from Ian Drake. To think anything else was too disturbing. More to prove this point than to test it, Maggie requested an appointment with him. She argued to herself that her plan for working after her marriage had to be discussed.

Ian Drake greeted her with formal courtesy, standing up but staying behind his desk. At his invitation Maggie settled herself comfortably, pleased with the self-confident poise she was maintaining. Ian Drake was simply her boss. She was here as his employee and there was nothing personal between them. His expression was remote, as unreadable as it had been at their first meeting in this office. She faced him calmly and proceeded to explain what she had in mind.

'There's a matter I want to discuss with you, Mr Drake, or perhaps I should say it's something I'd like you to consider.'

'Go on,' he invited smoothly.

'As you know, I'm getting married in February. I don't want to give up work, but I'm going to have a problem with time, travelling to begin with, and I expect to have a family eventually. It's not really practical or fair to expect Dan to travel, particularly since he has night-calls to the hospital. I'd like to be able to work at home, only coming into the office when it's necessary. I wondered if something could be worked out along those lines.'

'I don't see why not. I presume you mean on a sub-contract basis. You can say yes or no to an account, according to your time limitations. That's what you need, isn't it?'

'Yes.'

He nodded. Then suddenly his eyes were piercing hers, projecting satisfaction. 'I wondered which way you'd jump. This is a better course than opening your own agency. You have our whole organisation on tap at your convenience.'

'And you keep my talent on tap,' she pointed out.

'A fair exchange,' he agreed with a faint smile.

'I'm glad you think so.'

His gaze fell, fixing on his hands which lay spread on the desk. The unexpected silence became uncomfortable and Maggie began to wonder if there was more she should be saying.

He sighed and when he looked up his gaze locked forcefully on to hers.

'Does he know what he's getting, Maggie?'

She stared back at him. The knowledge in his eyes writhed around her soul, impossible to deny. It was as if she was mentally stripped naked and it was futile to try and hide.

'Not really,' she heard herself say in a strained voice.

'I didn't think so. You were surprised that morning in the elevator, as if you couldn't believe anyone else understood.' He slumped back in his chair, surveying her more softly, sympathetically. 'It's harder for a woman. There are more demands made on them from husband and children. A man has the role of breadwinner, so he's expected to work anyway. Will he give you the leeway you need?'

'I think so,' she answered stiffly.

He had intertwined the fingers of both hands across his broad chest and he watched his thumbs revolve around each other as he spoke. 'I asked you last week, but I thought you answered too quickly, so pardon me for asking again. I'd like to know.' His gaze sliced across to her, compelling in its insight. 'Are you happy with him?'

A surge of resentment sent blood racing up her neck. He could see her vulnerability and was pecking at it mercilessly. 'Why?' she flared at him, grey eyes flashing daggers above the fire on her cheeks. 'Why do you want to know? You shouldn't want to know. It's none of your business!'

'You're a high-flyer, Maggie—we both know that. You need a safe anchor when you climb down. Does he provide it?' he asked, relentlessly boring into her.

'Does Pat?' she defended bluntly.

It had been instinctive, this hurling of the challenge back at him, stabbing blindly at his veneer of confidence, wanting him to feel the same painful uncertainty she felt. A guarded look came into his eyes.

'My relationship with Pat is not in question. It satisfies my requirements,' he said with cool emphasis.

Maggie lost her cool completely. 'Then be satisfied! And keep your questions to yourself. My private life is not your province, Mr Drake.'

'It was you who brought it up,' he reminded her pointedly. 'You put forward a problem directly concerned with your forthcoming marriage. It should be clear to you that it won't be the only one. Think about it.' He leaned forward intently. 'Does he respect your need to express yourself? Does he love you enough not to mind your obsessiveness?'

'Stop it, damn you!' Maggie was on her feet, gesticulating wildly. 'Of course he loves me. Why do you think he's marrying me?'

Ian Drake pushed himself upright and for the first time his expression revealed emotion, a taut anger which lashed out in impatient words as he rounded the desk and confronted her. 'Don't tell me you don't see the obvious, Maggie—you're too intelligent to be that blind. Most men would see you as a prize, a beautiful thing to possess. Only you're not a thing.' His eyes burned down at her, scorching through to her soul, commanding her attention far more than the hand which caressed her smooth cheek. 'This beauty is a distraction, a surface layer which hides the real you. I've seen you in action, Maggie. You think I don't recognise the pulse underneath, driving you on to achieve. What'll happen if he wants you to stop?'

'Why are you speaking to me like this? Why?' she whispered urgently, her whole body trembling at his nearness and the strong intimacy he was projecting.

He sighed. His eyes softened and his hand dropped to her shoulder, giving it a gentle squeeze. 'You and I . . . we're cut from the same mould, Maggie. If I don't speak to you, who will? Who else knows? A marriage where your husband's needs will war against yours would be a bad mistake. You'd be torn in two.'

That was exactly what Ian Drake was doing, rending away the protective covering she had grown over the last few days. She shut her eyes as the pain of loneliness poured through all the inner cracks. She drew in a shuddering breath and showed him her desolation. 'What the hell do you care? You've got your woman.'

Something intense and uncontrolled blazed out of his eyes, a mental fire which cauterised her wounds and sparked a compulsive yearning for more and more heat. His hand slid from her shoulder, reaching under her hair to the back of her neck, its grip slowly tightening. Maggie was not conscious of moving closer, and yet suddenly their bodies were touching. An arm was around her waist. The fine wool of his suit-coat was underneath her palms. Her lips quivered in anticipation as his mouth descended. The

moment was charged with a mesmerising mag-
netism and it seemed that nothing could stop this
drawing together.

Then abruptly the fire was quenched. His
eyelids snapped shut; his lips thinned into grim
lines. He jerked away from her as if tearing
himself out of an unhealthy trance. Maggie stared
after him, stunned by the rude shock of rejection.
Without a word he walked stiffly around to his
chair, gripping the back of it so tightly that his
knuckles shone whitely. He shook his head as if
in denial and she saw his chest expand as he drew
in a deep breath.

'Madness!' The word was barely audible,
escaping from his lips as he pulled himself
together. When he finally met her gaze his eyes
seemed opaque, impenetrable, all defences in
place. His words hit her sharply, like slaps on the
face.

'You're right—I've found the woman I need.
She's everything I want. I hope Dan's the right
man for you. I'm sorry, I shouldn't have upset
you. You're right about that, too—it's not my
business. My concern stemmed from a strong
dislike of seeing your kind of talent ruined by a
destructive relationship. But that's your choice. I
have no right to interfere. Please overlook my . . .
my stupidity. I'll draw up a sample contract for
you and we can discuss it before your marriage
takes place. I'm sure we can reach an agreement
which will be satisfactory to both you and the
Agency.'

Maggie felt choked. Whatever it was that had
leapt to life between them was strangling in coils
of despair. Her eyes accused him of its murder.

Without a word she spun on her heel and walked out like a zombie who had lost its soul.

She went home the next weekend intending to break her engagement. Dan deflected her attempts, using a mixture of soft persuasion and sexual distraction to weaken her arguments. He telephoned her frequently the following week, even travelling into the city one night to take her out. Maggie was kept afloat with his devotion. He semi-filled a void she was too frightened to face. She recognised her compliance as weakness, but the habit of Dan was proving too difficult to break without help, and there was no help. Her mother sided with Dan, unable to understand her daughter's doubts. Ian Drake had pointed at the shaky foundations of a marriage to Dan, but the only alternative he had given her was a vacant block.

The Christmas social season started early and built momentum. Every weekend Maggie and Dan were invited to dinner parties, barbecues, poolside brunches. It was all very convivial, leaving them little time alone. She drifted along with the tide, hiding the inner fear and loneliness.

Even at work everyone was looking forward to the Agency's annual party. Each Christmas a large conference room was hired in a nearby hotel. It was always a lively affair, set out in cabaret style with a huge buffet meal laid on and a band to provide music for dancing. The hotel decked the room out in balloons, streamers and the usual Christmas decorations. It was the main topic of conversation at work for the whole week preceding it.

'Guess what?' Rhonda pounced on Maggie, first thing on the Monday morning.

'What?' she smiled obligingly.

'My new boy-friend said he'd come to our Christmas party. And Maggie—he's an absolute dream of a dancer!' She hugged herself and pirouetted around excitedly.

'Good for you,' Maggie laughed. 'Is he promising husband material?'

'I don't know yet, but he sure knows how to get my blood tingling! What about Dan? Is he coming in?'

'Yes, he'll be there.'

Rhonda wrinkled her nose. 'I wonder who Peter Cameron will bring. Remember that toffee-nosed tart last year?'

'She wasn't a tart. She was a model, you idiot,' Maggie corrected her with a droll look.

'Well, she dressed like a tart. What are you going to wear? How about coming shopping with me and we'll buy something new. We could go through some of the boutiques at lunchtime and really do ourselves proud.'

'Okay, why not? It might give me a lift.'

'Do you need one? Come to think of it, you haven't looked too bright lately. Anything wrong, Maggie?'

She shook her head, rejecting the impulsive kindness on Rhonda's face. 'Just end-of-year blues, probably. A new dress will cure me.'

'You know who I'm looking forward to seeing?' Rhonda bubbled on, easily reassured.

Maggie shrugged.

'Ian Drake's fiancée.'

'Yes, it should be quite interesting,' Maggie said flatly.

'They're getting married in April.'

'I know.'

'You know? Why didn't you tell me?'

'I didn't think it was any great news.'

'Honestly, Maggie! You know I find him positively fascinating,' Rhonda claimed in mild exasperation.

'What about the new boy-friend?' Maggie teased.

'That's different. He's my league. Ian Drake's something else again. You never tell me anything about him, and you see him often enough.'

'Enough to know I don't want to see him often,' Maggie said wryly. 'Skip it, Rhonda. I've got work to do. I'll see you at lunch-time.'

Patricia Hollis carried her own fascination for Maggie. She wanted to meet the woman who was right for Ian Drake, the one who would fulfil all his needs. Yes, she was curious about her, but she was glad Dan would be standing at her side. Maggie's composure was very brittle these days. She steered clear of Ian Drake at the office. Any necessary meeting with him was kept strictly businesslike. He had made no more personal comments to disturb her and she barely met his eyes even when he spoke to her. However, her carefully constructed composure received an unexpected knock on Thursday afternoon, when Rhonda breezily informed her that Ian Drake required Maggie's presence in his office, as of now.

There was no business pending, nothing to require his immediate interest, and Maggie felt vaguely apprehensive as she made her way upstairs. She did not want to be alone with Ian Drake. A growing tension stiffened her normally graceful movements.

His smile of greeting eased the strain on her nerves. He invited her to sit down and handed her a slip of paper.

'Your bonus for the Jamieson campaign. I hope you find it satisfactory?'

Maggie glanced down at the printed figures. 'Yes, thank you. Apparently the Company was very satisfied,' she observed dryly. The bonus was far more than she had expected.

He grinned. 'I understand that all sales records have been broken. Tigatom really hit the market.'

Instead of returning to his chair he had propped himself against the desk, barely a metre from her.

'Yes. Well, I'm glad it worked so well,' she muttered, over-conscious of his closeness. 'Is that all, Mr Drake?' A tight note had crept into her voice and she looked up warily, hoping he had not noticed.

A quick frown marred his smooth demeanour and then he was nodding. 'Yes . . . yes, that's all. I wanted you to know that the Agency appreciates the high calibre of your work.'

'That's very kind of you.' Maggie stood up, preparing to go.

'Are you and Dan attending the Christmas party tomorrow night?' The tone was casual, almost too casual.

She looked at him sharply, but his expression was bland. 'Yes,' she answered briefly.

'I shall be interested to meet your fiancé.'

Unaccountably tears filled her eyes. A painful

surge of emotion constricted her chest. She turned blindly and headed for the door, desperately needing to get away from him before she shamed herself by breaking down.

'Maggie . . .'

It was a question, an order to stay, a cry of concern. Her hand was on the knob but she did not turn it. She closed her eyes and bent her head, resting her forehead against the door as she struggled to regain control of herself. A hand fell lightly on her shoulder, tentative in its touch.

'Is something wrong?'

She blinked rapidly and lifted her head, turning it slightly in his direction but not meeting his enquiring gaze. 'Is anything right?' she retorted with a twist of irony.

The hand on her shoulder squeezed the soft flesh. 'Your work is.'

She looked at him then, the tear-washed grey eyes showing all the greyness of her inner loneliness. 'Is that enough, Ian?'

His hand dropped away. His body seemed to tense and the softness she had glimpsed in his eyes was replaced by hard determination.

'You can only trust what you create yourself. That's where satisfaction lies. It's the only satisfaction worth having because it lasts, and it's under your own control.'

'What if there's something you can't control? What do you do when there's a need in you crying out to be fulfilled, and the one person who might fulfil it turns away from you?'

It was a cry from the soul, a spontaneous protest against his coldness. For a moment his control slipped and a flicker of naked yearning peered out of the black depths of his eyes.

'Ian . . .'

It was a desperate plea and Maggie's hand reached out, instinctively drawn to touch him. Her feet moved of their own accord, taking a step closer. The conflict of will against desire showed clearly on Ian Drake's face. Then with a shuddering expulsion of breath he gathered her in and his mouth was on hers, as greedy to taste what she was offering as she was to receive what he could give.

It was a kiss that shattered all Maggie's preconceptions of what a kiss could be, so draining in its impact that her need was his, and the hungry longing which surged between them was a vibrant, compelling demand. Their bodies strained closer. Hands moved in avid possession.

Then suddenly Ian wrenched his mouth away from hers, his breath coming in harsh gasps. 'No—this is crazy! Crazy. I didn't mean to do this.' He thrust her away from him, his fingers biting into her upper arms. 'I'm sorry, I shouldn't have . . .' He shook his head in urgent denial. 'Please forgive me.'

Her lips were still throbbing with sensitivity, her heart pounding with the desire to be one with him. Her eyes searched his feverishly, silently begging him to take her in his arms again. He sucked in a sharp breath and stepped away, a deliberate step of rejection. Maggie sagged back against the door, needing support as a chilling weakness swept through her.

'Why?' It was an accusation hurled out of despair.

He flinched as it hit its mark. 'I don't want you, Maggie.' The words were grated out, flint-like in their hard sharpness.

A hysterical little laugh bubbled out of her throat. Then she clamped her mouth shut, biting her lips in an effort to steady herself. When she spoke it was a harsh croak. 'That's not what it felt like just then.'

He made an impatient gesture, his eyes angry coals, the flame of desire determinedly quenched. 'You're not what I want. You're a very desirable woman . . . but you're not what I want. Do you understand?'

'No, I don't understand,' Maggie retorted fiercely. 'How can you . . .'

'Because I choose,' he cut in swiftly, not letting her remind him of what was undeniable. 'I choose to control my life and I don't choose to have you disordering it.'

'Disordering it?' Maggie repeated incredulously. Ian Drake had well and truly disordered her life. It was falling around her in pieces and never would she be able to pick them up again in the same pattern. 'Do you know I can't even think straight because of you? For weeks I've been going through the motions of living, but I haven't been alive. I only felt alive when you . . .'

'No!' He snapped the word at her, then walked around his desk and sat down, separating himself from her as decisively as possible.

Maggie stared at him, seeing the grim set of his face and slowly accepting that he meant what he said. 'I see,' she nodded, forcing a calmness she did not feel. 'That wasn't important to you. That was just a kiss you'd give to any desirable woman who threw herself at you.'

His lips thinned even further, but his gaze wavered from hers. He leaned forward and snatched up a pencil. His face was brooding with repressed emotion as he twisted the smooth wood between his fingers. 'You know you're far more than that,' he said grudgingly. 'But you're like me, Maggie, and you can't keep two piranhas in a bowl. They'd devour each other.'

'Maybe I want to be devoured,' Maggie said slowly.

His eyes flashed up at her, fierce with resentment. 'Well, I don't. I've fought too hard to carve out my own identity, and now I want a pleasant, regular family background where I can relax and be content. I'm going to marry Pat.'

Maggie felt as if she had been slapped in the face with a wet towel. 'You don't love her . . .' she stated in cold retaliation, '. . . any more than I love Dan.'

'I am going to marry her. And you're quite wrong—I do love Pat.'

The words were spoken with deadly emphasis and his eyes stabbed home the ultimate rejection. Maggie felt a savage pain in her heart. Her lashes fluttered down, veiling her anguish. A crumpled piece of paper lay on the carpet near her feet. She bent down and picked it up, her hands automatically smoothing out the bonus cheque.

'Well, I do have my work,' she muttered derisively. 'Thank you for the cheque, Mr Drake. It was very generous of you.'

Giving him no time to reply, she swiftly opened the door and stepped out, closing it firmly behind her. She now knew what it was like to drop from heaven to hell in one fell swoop. Her whole being writhed at the loss, at her inability to climb back to what had been closed off so wilfully, damning her to outer darkness.

She groped her way back downstairs and walked blindly through the maze of partitions to her private little cubicle. Gradually her eyes focused on her desk, then moved slowly to her drawing-board. Her brain told her she was lucky. Not many people had work they enjoyed. Her life was not pointless. Ian Drake was right: there was satisfaction in her work. Of course she could not marry Dan. That had now become impossible. But perhaps there would be another man, some time in the future. After all, she was a very desirable woman.

Tears sprang to her eyes as Ian Drake's words echoed through her mind, hollow, tinny words which mocked her attempt at positive thinking. She dashed the tears away and forced herself to start work again. She achieved very little, but it filled in the afternoon. She did not know how to fill the other holes in her life.

# CHAPTER FOUR

'MAGGIE love, I'm sorry to disappoint you, but I can't come in to your party tonight. Mrs Arnold's multiple birth is on the way and I have to stand by.'

'That's all right, Dan. I understand,' Maggie replied flatly. She had not wanted to go to the party with him anyway, pretending everything was all right when it was all wrong. Her engagement to him had to be broken this weekend, firmly and irrevocably. She wished she could do it over the telephone now, but Dan deserved more courtesy than that.

'You sound really let down. I'm sorry, darling, but I can't order nature. Would it be too ghastly to go on your own? After all, you do know everyone. It's not as if it would be awkward mixing in.'

'No, honestly, it doesn't really matter to me,' she insisted, trying to inject lightness into her tone. 'I'll come home on the train. Now you go off and deliver healthy babies and I'll see you tomorrow. Okay?'

'Okay. Thanks for being so understanding. I love you.'

She could not reciprocate the words, not any more. ''Bye, Dan,' she sighed, and put the telephone down. Tomorrow she had to finish it, hand his ring back. It had been weak and dishonest of her to keep him dangling this long.

It was almost five o'clock. She tidied her desk, picked up her handbag and strolled listlessly towards the elevator. The doors opened. Bert Oliver was casually propped against the back wall.

'Hi, Maggie! Why so glum, chum?'

'No party for me. Dan's stuck with a multiple birth,' she answered glibly.

'Rot! Do you mean to say you'd turn your back on our once-a-year do just because the Greek god can't be with you?' he demanded mockingly. 'Don't the rest of us rate?'

'Come on, Bert!' she shot back at him. 'You know what it's like on your own.'

His eyes narrowed on her bleak expression. 'Too true, dear girl, too true. Tell you what— come to the party and sit with me. We'll make merry together and thumb our noses at everyone else.' A sly twinkle enlivened his eyes. 'Just think what a turn-up for the books that'd be, the office fairy with the most gorgeous woman at the whole shebang! Why, you'd grace my arm like it's never been graced before!'

She raised a quizzical eyebrow at him as the elevator doors opened on to the ground floor. He grabbed her arm and led her out, almost prancing with puckish delight.

'What a lovely idea! Can't you see their faces? Peter Cameron's will be green! It's so perfectly perverse, you with me. Oh, do come, Maggie— it'll be a real lark. You won't even miss Dan at all, I promise you.'

She stopped walking and looked at him, suddenly attracted by the mad idea. Bert was capable of making the party fun in his own inimitable way, and Maggie was tempted by another reason altogether. She wanted to see Pat Hollis, the woman Ian Drake was intent on marrying. It was a stupid, self-destructive impulse which could only give her pain, but the need to see, to know, to understand this so-called love was suddenly overwhelming.

'All right, Bert. Save me a seat next to you.'

He whirled her around and drew her into a crazy tango step across the lobby. 'Oh, we'll trip the light fantastic, breathe in bubbly and drum up a storm of laughter, Maggie, me darlin'. We'll have us a ball!'

They reached the main doorway and he let her go. Maggie could not help laughing at his mad antics. Other people in the lobby had bemused looks on their faces, but she did not care. Bert had made her feel better.

He waved an admonishing finger at her. 'Mind you look your most beautiful, glamorous best. I'll dig out my tux and come all formal and dignified. Why, just for you, Maggie, I'll pretend I'm almost straight. It appeals to my sense of the ridiculous.'

'I think I'm catching the mood,' Maggie grinned at him. 'We'll put everyone else in the shade. Right?'

'Right!' he agreed with smug satisfaction, wriggling his fingers at her as she waved him goodbye.

Maggie carried out Bert's instructions with meticulous attention to detail. Pride demanded that she look her best if she was putting in an appearance. Her fingernails were manicured and varnished a pearly opal. She played up her eyes with violet and silver eyeshadow. A string of baroque pearls drew attention to the low V-neckline of her dress and glowed lustrously on the soft swell of breasts. The mauve chiffon of the bodice darkened to a midnight purple at the hem of the skirt and silver sandals completed an outfit which was the essence of femininity. She splashed a liberal amount of Arpège around her throat and then telephoned for a taxi.

As it happened Bert was standing on the pavement outside the hotel when she arrived. His eyes sparkling with impish humour, he hooked her arm in his and swept her inside, mouthing extravagant compliments until Maggie was bubbling with laughter. Bert himself looked quite distinguished in his tuxedo. His customary style of dress tended to be flamboyant, but tonight even his manner was schooled to the occasion. He played the role of escort with distinction while his tongue tripped out wickedly apt comments about the whole company.

They loaded a tray with various delicacies from the buffet and Bert commandeered a bottle of champagne before they settled at a corner table. From there they could view the crowd and chat at leisure. Most of the women were dissected with bitchy glee, Bert saving his most delicious comments for Peter Cameron's lady of the evening. He suddenly broke off with a whistle of interest.

'So that's Drake's choice!'

Maggie followed his line of vision, her heart fluttering with a nervous skip. Pat Hollis had a round, vivacious face, pretty without having any pretensions to beauty. Her honey-gold hair was beautifully styled in a swirling cap around her head. She was not short enough to be called petite, but her figure was slight, her movements graceful. Her skin had a lovely golden tan which set off the simple white dress she wore.

'What's your verdict, Maggie? You've had a long enough squiz,' Bert prompted.

'He has good taste. I think she looks quite lovely,' she admitted slowly.

'Yep. A nice bit of fluff, all right,' he agreed irreverently. 'Hullo, hullo, hullo! Drake's frowning at us. Bet he's surprised to see me monopolising you, my sweet. Now he's scanning the room, checking everyone out. Bet he works in his sleep, that guy.'

'Well, he obviously doesn't work all the time,' Maggie remarked sardonically.

'Nope. Must have taken some time off to get himself a woman. I wonder how she copes with him switching off.'

Maggie frowned. 'Why do you say that?'

'Don't frown, sweetie—gives you unsightly wrinkles. Haven't you ever seen him concentrate on a problem? He's like a terrier with a bone. A lot like you, as a matter of fact, a fanatic for attention to detail, ruddy perfectionist.' The band tuned up and Bert switched his attention to the lead guitarist as they swung into an upbeat number. 'There's fancy Fred. Well, what do you know! Come on, Maggie. We'll pitter-patter around the floor and I'll wink at him. Bet he misses a note.'

He was a good dancer and Maggie enjoyed his exuberance as he threw himself into the rhythm. She blocked Ian Drake out of her mind and gave

herself up to the physical pleasure of the dance.
Greetings were exchanged as couples moved past.
Dan's absence was questioned and answered,
seriously by Maggie, flippantly by Bert. They
were both ready to slake their thirst by the time
the bracket finished.

'Mind our seats, Maggie. I'll hunt up another
bottle of Champers.'

She nodded, content to sit and rest her feet. A
sharp sense of loneliness swept through her. She
twisted the sapphire ring around her finger,
thinking of Dan and wondering whether any or
all of the triplets had been born yet.

'Maggie?'

She glanced up guardedly at the sound of Ian
Drake's voice. Her gaze sliced to the woman at
his side. She was smiling at Maggie, lovely blue
eyes ready to be pleased.

'Hello,' Maggie said automatically.

'Maggie Tarrington, Pat Hollis.'

Both women ignored the man, each curious
about the other.

'I've been so interested to meet you, Maggie. I
loved your toy ads,' said Pat with sincere
admiration.

'Thank you. It was fun doing them.'

'Ian didn't mention you were beautiful as well
as talented.' She cast a chiding look up at her
fiancé. 'Are you blind or something?'

'Did it matter?' he said carelessly.

'Oh, you men!' Pat grinned at Maggie.
'They're quite impossible, aren't they?'

'Sometimes,' she agreed with an ironic little
smile.

'Dan not here, Maggie?'

The soft question stabbed at her heart. She could not bring herself to look at him. She directed her explanation to his fiancée. 'No. He was called into hospital to attend a multiple birth. Bert . . .'

'Ta-ta-ta!' Bert suddenly reappeared, flourishing a bottle of champagne and four glasses. 'I saw the boss and his lady were here and brought you all a glass. Let's toast the season.' He poured with gay abandon, barely pausing to acknowledge the introduction to Pat Hollis. 'Ah yes, Miss Hollis. Maggie and I decided that your fiancé has good taste.'

'Bert!' Maggie gasped in embarrassment.

Pat laughed and accepted the glass he offered her. 'Thank you. You have very good taste yourself.'

'Oh, Maggie's not mine,' he said blithely. 'I'm standing in for her regular Adonis who's off delivering babies ad infinitum.'

Pat looked puzzled. 'I'm sorry, I seem to have lost the thread somewhere.'

'Maggie's fiancé is a gynaecologist,' Ian Drake explained.

'Oh, what bad luck he was called out tonight,' Pat said sympathetically.

'Aha! But my very good luck,' Bert declared grandly.

'Does this happen very often?' Pat persisted to Maggie.

'Not really.'

'It's a wonder it happens at all,' Bert scoffed. 'He's so handsome it's sinful. If I ever had a wife, God forbid, the last doctor I'd send her to would be Dan Barlow!'

'You must make a very striking couple,' Pat observed, and there was a hint of relief in her smile.

'I think you've both got Maggie totally embarrassed. Let's drink to a very good year,' Ian Drake suggested with a touch of impatience.

They all repeated the toast and Maggie almost drained her glass. She felt Ian Drake's eyes on her and defensively finished the lot.

'Thirsty?' he queried softly.

'Yes.' She flicked a polite glance at him, evading his searching gaze by sliding her eyes to his fiancée. 'Ad people are all slightly mad, you know. You have to make allowances. Bert here loves pulling everybody's legs and I'm known to be . . .'

'A steamroller,' Bert supplied emphatically. 'She winds up and pity anyone who gets in her way! She looks beautiful and fragile, but there's pure steel inside, totally inflexible. She has to have her way. You should try sketching for her sometimes. It's just that I have such a lovely nature that I put up with her. And of course, the minor fact that she's always right has its points too. You know that cat in the toy ads? I swear I drew its tail twenty times before she was satisfied.'

'But, Bert . . .' Maggie expostulated.

'I know, I know.' He waved his hands expressively. 'It had just the right flick in the final sketch.'

They all laughed at his clever mimic of the cat.

'I'll take a special look at that tail next time I see the toy ads,' Pat assured him appreciatively.

Fortunately the band started up again and

Maggie breathed a sigh of relief as Ian Drake
steered his fiancée elsewhere. She gestured for
Bert to refill her glass, then drank the contents
quickly to ease her dry throat.

'Steady on, me girl! The night is young. What
is it with you two? He watches you like a hawk
and you won't look at him.'

'It's nothing, Bert,' she shrugged carelessly.

'Who's kidding who, sweetie? You might have
fooled pretty Pat, but the eye of an artist is not so
easily deceived.'

'Drop it!' she flared, and reached for the bottle.

He gripped her hand and shook his head. 'Uh-
uh, Maggie. We'll dance and put on a perform-
ance, you and me, and no one will see into our
black souls.'

Bert set himself to make her unwind, forcing
her around the dance-floor and chivvying her
back into a relaxed mood. They bumped into
Rhonda and her new boy-friend and spent the
next break with them. Peter Cameron then
claimed Maggie for a dance. He set her teeth on
edge and when he finally released her, Maggie
was more than ready for another drink.

Bert's interest was obviously engaged elsewhere
and she sat in her corner with her face turned
away from the crowd. She thought of Dan,
comparing him to Pat Hollis. They were nice
people, both of them. She felt quite sure Ian
Drake would have liked Dan as much as she liked
Pat. The problem was in herself, not Dan. She
was unaware of time passing, unaware of how
many drinks she sipped. There was too much
sorting out to be done in her mind.

'Maggie, would you like to dance?'

She lifted her eyes to Ian Drake without bothering to veil her misery. 'No, thank you,' she said very distinctly and turned away.

He slid into Bert's seat but she concentrated her gaze on her glass, idly tipping it backwards and forwards. 'Go away,' she said quietly. 'Go back to your fiancée.'

'She's dancing. You're drinking too much, Maggie.'

'I like her.'

He paused. 'Everybody likes Pat,' he said tonelessly. 'I would have been interested to meet Dan.'

'You'll never meet Dan.'

'Why not?'

'You would have only met him through me, and that's finished. I can't do it.'

'Can't do what?'

'I can't marry him. I've been sitting here thinking it over. I've been so weak and stupid and now I'm going to hurt him.' She shook her head slowly, aware of a slight fuzziness. 'Poor Dan,' she sighed.

'You're getting morose, Maggie. Come and dance.'

He took the glass from her hands and pulled her to her feet before she could make an effective protest.

'I don't want to dance with you,' she mumbled into his shoulder as he swung her against him.

'Pretend it's Dan if you like,' he replied coolly. 'And don't be a goddamned fool, Maggie. Just because he couldn't make it tonight there's no reason to turn him down.'

'You know that's not the reason!' she hissed, angry with his deliberate obtuseness.

They circled the dance-floor in silence and she was conscious of every muscle in his body, the slow tempo of the music demanding close physical contact for dancing. Ian's shorter stature was more comfortable to her body than Dan's taller frame. He tensed as she moved closer, but Maggie was letting herself dream of forbidden things.

'Why, then?' he suddenly breathed in her ear, his whisper carrying a sharp urgency.

'I've tasted something else, haven't I?' she mocked. He was evading the truth which she had finally faced. 'Maybe there's another man for me somewhere. Better nothing than to keep up a pretence. Don't talk—I don't want to talk. You obviously have nothing to say to me. You had no right to say anything to me in the first place.' Tears welled up in her eyes and she blinked them away. 'I feel so lonely.'

His hold tightened for a moment, then relaxed. He said nothing. They circled the floor in a numb silence until the music ended. Ian led her back to the table where Bert was once more ensconced in their corner. He waved another full bottle of champagne at her and she forced a grin.

'Well done, Bert. Thank you, Mr Drake,' she added politely as he let go her arm.

'Take it easy, Maggie,' he muttered, and left her.

Bert poured out a drink. 'Here's to inter-office relations! May they ever be so interesting,' he smirked.

'And here's to the eye of the artist! May it

blink now and then,' she retorted wryly, and they drank.

A long time later they were sitting with their heads propped against the wall, watching the crowd grow thin.

'Are you trying to drink me under the table, Maggie me girl?' Bert rolled out in a sonorous tone.

'What? And put a stain on your peerless reputation? Never!' she declared pompously.

'You're a woman of steel.'

'Slightly molten around the edges.'

'Did I ever tell you about the time I was up before a judge, Maggie? They're terribly sober. He didn't like my tie.'

Maggie giggled. Bert was notorious for his outrageous ties. 'I like your ties, Bert. They're very individual.'

'Paint them myself. Is that pretty Pat popping up?'

Pat Hollis suddenly appeared and took hold of Maggie's arm. 'Come on, Maggie, we're taking you home. Ian's gone for the car. I'll help you out.'

'Don't want help. I don't need help, do I, Bert?' she appealed to him.

'Woman of steel,' he repeated knowingly.

'Please, Maggie. Ian's worried about you. Please come with me.'

'You go with him. You belong together. Not me. I'm on my own,' Maggie insisted with a shake of her head which set her senses swimming.

'Bert, you persuade her to come,' Pat said anxiously.

'Better go, Maggie. Boss's girl. Inter-office relations, you know.'

'Why me? Why pick on me?' she muttered resentfully. 'I'm sitting here minding my own business.'

'Dan's not here. Drake probably thinks I'm not responsible enough. Wrong, you know—I'm very responsible.' He waved a careless hand. 'Who cares why? You get a free trip home. Go on, go with Pat. She wants you to be a good girl.'

'Good girl?' She gave a hysterical peal of laughter. 'Oh, Bert! You wouldn't believe what a good girl I am.'

'Shut up, Maggie!'

Ian Drake's grim voice silenced her. She was walked like a puppet out of the hotel and bundled into his car. Her head lolled back on the cold leather seat and tears streamed uncontrollably down her cheeks. Humiliation was a huge lump in her throat. She was being driven home by the man she wanted while the woman he wanted sat beside him, a silent witness to Maggie's distress.

The car stopped. She opened the door and stumbled out. Ian Drake caught her and supported her as he steered her into the apartment building. He took her to the right door and propped her against the wall while he found her key in her handbag.

'How did you know my address?' Maggie asked dully.

'Personnel file.'

'So damned clever!'

He opened the door. Maggie pushed past him and slammed it in his face. She just made it to the bathroom before retching violently, her whole body racked with convulsions which kept her heaving upwards. When her stomach was totally emptied, she flushed the basin and slumped down on the tiled floor, too weak to move.

Then she cried, great, noisy sobs, weeping for something she never had and which seemed forever out of her reach. She cried for Dan, for her mother, but mostly for herself, until she had no more tears to shed. The tiles were cold and her body felt stiff and sluggish. She dragged herself up and washed the sick taste out of her mouth, then brushed her teeth. She felt dirty all over. Very slowly, fumbling with fingers which still trembled, she stripped off her clothes, intent on having a shower. She was just reaching to turn on the taps when the bathroom door was pushed open and she stared at Ian Drake, rigid with shock.

His eyes were dark pools of pain as he stared back at her. 'I thought ... I was afraid ... Are you all right, Maggie?'

She jerked out of her trance, suddenly aware of her nakedness. 'Oh God!' she whispered. 'Haven't you seen enough?'

He stepped forward and crushed her to him, so tightly that buttons on his shirt bit into her flesh. 'I couldn't stand the silence,' he muttered hoarsely, dragging his fingers through her hair, stroking her back with a roughness that was both pleasure and pain.

She could not believe this was happening and she tilted her head back to question. His eyes glittered feverishly and then his mouth took hers with almost savage demand. It was no sensual exploration but a passionate possession as if he could not bear for any part of her to escape him.

Maggie instinctively gave him everything he

asked, responding with a wild, insatiable need of
her own, feeding the violence of his emotion with
all the craving of her heart. They were both
breathing raggedly when he finally dragged his
mouth away from hers. He pressed her head into
the curve of his throat while he rocked her in a
fierce embrace. Maggie wasn't sure if the shudder
which trembled through them was his or her
own.

'Why do you do this to me?' he groaned,
turning his face to rub each cheek against her hair
in an agony of need. 'I could hardly bear to sit
through that wretched weeping, but the silence
. . . I had to know. I'm sorry, Maggie.'

She was too dazed to take it in. All she knew
was that his arms were around her and she clung
like a limpet around his neck, not wanting him to
ever let her go. She did not know how he was
here or why he was here. The incredible reality
was that he was holding her and she wanted him
to go on holding her for ever. She gave a little
moan of protest as he unclasped her hands and
drew her arms down. He eased her away from
him, looking down at her with tender concern.

'Come on, Maggie, have your shower. That's
what you were going to do, wasn't it?'

She stared at him dumbly, unable to order any
coherent thought. He kept one arm supporting
her while he reached out and turned on the taps,
feeling the water and adjusting it to the right
temperature. She saw his shirt-sleeve getting wet.
Then he was steering her under the stinging
spray and she gasped as the water hit her. He
kept a steadying hand on her shoulder for a
moment and then let go.

'I'll make us some coffee.'

The water beat down on her head and shoulders and she wondered vaguely if she had dreamed Ian Drake was here. She touched her lips, recalling the feel of his mouth. She glanced down at her body and saw the fading impression of a button on her breast. It had not been a dream. Her mind was too befogged to grasp it properly, to examine the whys and the wherefores. He was here, looking after her, caring for her with an intensity of feeling which completely obliterated the fact that she was naked. Her nakedness was irrelevant. He cared for her as a person.

Then he was back, turning off the taps and wrapping a towel around her, drying her, forcing her limp arms into a bathrobe and tying it securely around her waist. Water dripped from her hair and he towelled off the excess moisture. He looked down at her with a wry smile.

'You're a mess, Maggie, but I can't do any more for you. Do you want to comb your hair?'

She looked up at him with huge, lost eyes, too frightened to look for answers. He might go away if she spoke.

'Oh, to hell with it. You'll do,' he sighed, then put an arm around her shoulders and walked her out to the living-room. 'Sit at the table. You can prop your head up with your hands. I'll bring out the coffee.'

Maggie did as she was told, relieved not to have to think. A mug of black, pungent liquid was placed in front of her, steam curling up in waves.

'It's strong and sweet. Might help sober you up.'

Ian drew out the chair at the end of the table and sat down. The silence between them was thick with unspoken words. Maggie sipped the coffee in small sips, slowly ordering her mind until she could not leave the questions any longer. She raked her damp hair, pushing it away from her face, then left her hands on her brow, shading the vulnerability in her eyes.

'Why are you here?'

He did not answer immediately. When he did speak his voice was flat and unemotional. 'You needed someone with you.'

She drew in a sharp, steadying breath and asked, 'How did you get in?'

'The key was still in the door when you slammed it shut. You weren't thinking too clearly, Maggie.' He sighed and slouched down in the chair, stretching out his legs. 'I sent Pat home in the car and came back.'

'Poor Pat,' she murmured, imagining the other girl's hurt and bewilderment at being dismissed for the sake of another woman.

'I'll iron it out with her tomorrow. You were breaking up, Maggie, and I couldn't take the risk of leaving you alone, not in the state you were in.'

She dragged her hands down her face and looked at him fully. There were lines of strain about his mouth, but what alarmed her most was the withdrawn look in his eyes. A sudden panic hit her. Ian was here, and yet . . .

'What do you mean, you'll iron it out with Pat tomorrow?' she asked tightly.

A carefully impassive mask settled over his

face. 'Don't get things out of perspective, Maggie. You needed help, but I love Pat and I'm going to marry her. Nothing has changed.'

'Nothing?' The question demanded that he justify his statement.

His mouth lifted into a wry twist. 'That was a mistake—a compassionate impulse, if you like. You would have felt worse if I'd turned away.'

'I suppose I should thank you. Dr Drake at work! A kiss in time saves sanity. You should have telephoned for Dan—he has more finesse,' she jabbed at him bitingly, hating him for this further rejection.

'Then keep his ring on your finger,' he retorted curtly.

She glanced down at the sapphire ring, drew it off and placed it on the table in front of them. 'I'm not as big a hypocrite as you are, Ian Drake.'

He sucked in his breath and stood up, rubbing the back of his neck as he stepped away from her. 'All right, I'm strongly attracted to you. Obviously I can't deny it. But it's too strong. Look what you're doing to me!' He swung around and resentment burnt in every tense line of his body. 'I'm here, nursemaiding you instead of being with Pat.'

'And making love to me,' she reminded him with equal passion. 'And don't say you didn't want to, Ian.'

Hatred leapt into his eyes. 'I don't want to, damn you! You're like a sickness I can't control, but don't think I like it, and don't think I won't fight it, because I'm not going to let you win, Maggie. I run my own life, and no one . . .'

He swallowed hard and turned his back on her,

pacing several steps before stopping abruptly. He squared his shoulders and she saw his chest heave up and down. When he faced her again he was in control.

'Look!' he said reasonably, one hand stretched out in appeal. 'I like you, Maggie, I respect the person that you are. I care enough about you to see that you come to no harm. But I do not want a close personal involvement with you.'

'Why not? Make me understand,' she demanded desperately. 'And don't throw Pat in my face, because your presence here makes nonsense of your so-called love for her. I love you, Ian, and . . .'

'Love!' He snarled the word contemptuously. 'You call that mindless passion love? How long would it last, Maggie? How long would you love me? How long would it be before your eyes turned elsewhere and . . .' He held up a clenched fist, then thrust his fingers out in a derisive gesture as he added, 'Poof goes love. Oh no, don't talk love to me!'

'You said you loved Pat,' she argued, completely bewildered by his vehement protest.

'Yes, I said that. I do love Pat, in a quiet, reasoned way. She's a good woman and I'm going to marry her. She'll be the kind of wife I want, and I'll provide her with every comfort her heart desires. I expect to have a very pleasant life with her. And if the time comes that Pat is discontented and wants something or someone else, I shall regret her going, very much. But it will not destroy me.'

Those last words were added with such a depth of bitterness that Maggie stared at him helplessly, appalled by the sterile life he had set for himself, and realising that something in the past had scarred this man so deeply, he would not let himself love. She licked lips which had suddenly gone very dry. Defeat was curling around her heart and somehow she had to find a way to combat the deadly coils.

'Ian, I want only you,' she began in a last, despairing appeal. 'I've waited so long . . .'

He was shaking his head as he approached her and she stopped speaking, knowing with utter certainty that words would not pierce his iron control.

'Don't keep on, Maggie.' His eyes appraised her coldly. 'You're all right now. Don't do anything hasty about Dan. Take your time and think it over. He could very well be the right husband for you.'

She jumped up, frantic to keep him from going. Her arms curled around his neck and she pressed her body to his, hoping that physical persuasion might bend his will. 'Please,' she whispered, and the word carried urgent longing, passionate with the memory of their brief intimacy.

For a moment Ian's heart thudded in unison with hers. Then he gently pushed her away, his hands firmly on her waist to prevent her repeating the tactic. 'No.' His eyes were hard with decision, not allowing a sliver of hope. 'I won't be tempted again. I'll leave you now. Go to bed and sleep it off.'

He strode towards the door and a hollow bereftness struck at her heart, making her sway with nausea. She gripped the back of the chair for support. 'You're running away,' she hurled after him bitterly.

He opened the door and looked back at her. 'No, I'm not running away. I'm taking the steps towards what I want. Positive steps, Maggie, not negative. I control my life; it's time you learnt to do the same. Goodnight.'

# CHAPTER FIVE

THE silence held an ominous quality. There was no acceptance, no resignation in Dan's demeanour. A little shiver of revulsion spread its coldness through Maggie's body. She did not want this scene prolonged any further; it had shredded her nerves. Compassion for Dan had already been stretched to its limits and she wanted, above all, to be left in peace to come to terms with her battered emotions.

She grimly reminded herself that Dan's departure would not bring peace anyway. Her mother had tactfully left them alone in the living-room in the fond belief that everything was as it should be, two people in love, shortly to be married. Maggie still had to disillusion her. Fay Tarrington would be shocked, disapproving, more likely to champion Dan's cause than to understand her daughter's position.

'Why?' It was a forceful demand, bursting out of a deep well of frustration.

'I've told you why, Dan,' Maggie replied with quiet insistence.

Dan's fist thumped down on the armrest of his chair as he stood up. 'A meaningless mumbo-jumbo of words!' he grated out in disgust, and began pacing the floor in front of her.

Maggie stared down at the dove-grey carpet, holding her tongue. She had given all the explanation she was prepared to give. Dan kept pacing like an angry tiger. Her eyes roved aimlessly around the tapestried chairs, the fondly polished antiques which gave an old-world elegance to her mother's living-room. It was not a room for impassioned outbursts. It was a room for refined good manners.

She tried again, softly, calmly. 'I'm sorry you don't understand, Dan, but . . .'

'You're mine! Mine!' he muttered savagely. 'Haven't I done everything you've asked? What more do you want, for God's sake? Just tell me!' He stopped in front of her, his fine, surgeon's hands stretched out in appeal. 'Tell me what I've done wrong!'

Maggie could not bear to look up at him. 'Please, Dan,' she sighed. 'You've done nothing wrong. You've been very good and patient with me, but . . .'

'Maybe that was my mistake,' he cut in harshly. He reached down and pulled her to her feet. She was held in a crushing embrace while one of his hands ran feverishly over her curves. 'Maybe this was what you wanted all along.' His mouth swooped on hers, greedy for possession, grinding the soft inner skin of her lips against teeth which denied him further intimacy. 'Damn you, Maggie!' he breathed in bitter defeat. 'I've had you quivering under my touch. You've responded to me—you know damned well you have. You can't cheat me now when I've waited so long!'

The wretched plea stabbed her with shame. She had clung on to Dan after her heart had told her it was dishonest. 'I'm sorry, I really am sorry. I should never have let it go on like this,' she whispered huskily. 'I didn't mean to hurt you, Dan . . .'

'Hurt me! All the nights I've lain awake tormented with the thought of you, wanting you so much I was almost out of my mind.' His hands gripped her shoulders with punishing strength. 'Look at me!'

His eyes were burning with an inner rage which had nothing to do with love. Maggie tried to shrink from him, but his fingers dug into her flesh, denying her movement.

'I've been patient—more patient than I'd be with any other woman. I'm not going to give you up, Maggie. This is just another of your temperamental fits of wavering. You don't know what you want, but I know this. You're going to be mine.'

'I'm not a possession, Dan. I'm a person with a mind of my own,' she stated tightly, beginning to resent his claims.

One hand released a shoulder and moved to grip her chin, forcing her to meet his gaze. 'That's just what you don't have, Maggie. You're a mass of neurotic fears, frightened of sex, frightened to have children, frightened to give up your work because it's the one thing you're confident about. Now I've pandered to your unrealistic whims, even conceded you the right to go on with your work for a while, though the last damned thing I want is a working wife . . .'

'Conceded! Conceded me the right! I have the right without any concession from you. I'm not your possession!' Maggie interrupted vehemently. 'You've just said it all, Dan.'

She tore herself out of his grasp and wheeled

around behind the armchair she had been sitting in, facing him across it, her expression set in defiant resolve. 'I don't want to argue with you any more. I've made up my mind and I want you to take back your ring. It's finished.'

He stared at her for a long, tense moment, fighting to gain control of his emotions. Then he bent and picked up the sapphire ring from the coffee-table where Maggie had placed it. He had refused to take it before. Now he held it so that the light caught the blue fire within. Then he flicked it into the air and caught it with a sharp, snatching movement. His eyes held an ironic gleam when he looked back at her.

'I'll keep it for you. It's obvious that there's no talking sense to you this afternoon. Have a breathing space if that's what you need, Maggie, but we're not finished. I'll call you.'

'Don't!'

He had already turned away from her and he kept walking.

'I won't answer, Dan,' she called after him, desperate to have the whole conflict behind her once and for all.

He paused in the doorway and glanced back at her mockingly. 'Yes, you will, Maggie. I've just worked it out. You're mad at me because I couldn't turn up at your precious office party last night. It was when I mentioned work that you went off like a rocket, but you'll get things back into perspective.'

'You're fooling yourself, Dan. It's over.'

'We'll see.' A tight grimness shadowed his face.

'I mean it,' Maggie bit out determinedly.

He shrugged and walked away. Maggie's

defiant bearing sagged and she closed her eyes as tears burned across them, hot with anger, frustration and a deep, deep despair. Dan's footsteps echoed on the tiles in the foyer. Fay Tarrington's voice called out, sharp with surprise, the words ending abruptly as the front door slammed shut.

Just let me be left alone, Maggie silently begged. Tears clustered behind her lids and squeezed out through her thick lashes. She groped her way around the chair she had clung to, slumped into it and covered her face with her hands. The emotional tension had exhausted her and even now there was no sense of relief, just an aching emptiness.

'Where's Dan off to, Maggie?' her mother asked as she entered the room. Her tone quickly changed to one of concern. 'Maggie? Is something wrong?'

There was no escape for her. Maggie dragged her hands down from her face and looked wearily at her mother. 'No, there's nothing wrong. Not now. I've ended what was wrong. Dan's gone because I finally had the courage to break our engagement.'

Her mother goggled at her, completely stunned. 'You did what?'

Maggie heaved a sigh, knowing she was in for another scene with her mother. She raised tired eyes and enunciated very clearly. 'I'm not marrying Dan and I gave him back his ring. It's finished, and you might as well accept it, Mum.'

It was too much for Fay Tarrington to accept. Maggie listened to a long, emotional tirade as her mother enumerated all the reasons why her daughter was insane. Eventually Fay Tarrington wound down, frustrated by the lack of any response.

'You'll never, never find another man as good as Dan,' she concluded, tight-lipped with disappointment. She threw up her hands in despair and sat down, her pose carrying an impatient expectancy.

'Probably not,' Maggie agreed listlessly, knowing there was only one way to get her mother off her back. 'You've said your piece, Mum, and now I'll tell you something. I won't discuss it, but I'll tell you because I don't want you preaching Dan at me any more. I love someone else. He's not free and he doesn't want me anyway, but I can't marry Dan because of what I feel for this man. I've been fighting it for weeks, but I know that if he turned to me I couldn't turn away. That's how it is, Mum, so don't say any more. It's hard enough to bear as it is.'

Fay Tarrington's face sagged as the stiff opposition drained out of it. Her body slumped forward, her hands shading her eyes as they propped up her head. A silent agony pervaded the room while both women took stock of the situation. At last Fay Tarrington looked up, her eyes moist and full of apology.

'I'm so sorry, dear. That's what you were trying to tell me the night you'd had too much to drink, and I didn't listen.' She shook her head in self-disgust. 'I should have listened. I thought you were just rambling.'

Maggie fought back her own tears, determined not to give in to self-pity. 'It doesn't matter, Mum. There's nothing you can do anyway. I just have to learn to live with it.'

'I've failed you,' her mother muttered, too distressed to remain silent.

'No. You wanted what you thought was best for me—I know that. I'm sorry I'm a disappointment to you.'

'Maggie, I only ever wanted your happiness. I thought Dan . . .' She stopped, biting her lips to hold back the words.

Maggie appreciated the effort at self-control. She sighed and gave her mother a wry smile. 'I know, Mum, but you can't order happiness.'

'This man . . . I suppose he's married?' The question was hesitant, wanting to tactfully elicit information but wary of giving pain.

'He's going to be.' Maggie plucked at the braid on the upholstered armrest of her chair. It was coming loose and she unconsciously made it worse before realising what she was doing. She stilled her fingers and looked across at her mother, a bleak desolation in her eyes. 'I thought last night there was a chance. He's been kind to me and I tried to use the situation. He . . . I threw myself at him and he turned me down flat.'

Her mother made to speak but Maggie shook her head. 'His fiancée is a very nice person—I actually like her. Funny, isn't it! I ought to hate her but I can't. For a little while last night I hated him . . . but I don't.' She lifted her hands in a hopeless little gesture. 'So there I am, Mum. I can't have him and I can't marry Dan. I guess your friends will inundate you with questions when they hear about the broken engagement. Please just say I changed my mind. It's the truth anyway. Okay?'

Fay nodded. 'I wish there was something I could do for you. I feel so . . . inadequate.'

Maggie drew in a long, shuddering breath and stood up. 'I think I'll go to my room. I didn't get much sleep last night and I need to be alone for a while. Don't worry,' she added quickly as her mother looked her anxiety, 'the worst is over. I'll cope. I feel too drained to talk any more.'

'All right, dear. Call me if you need anything.'

The weekend passed slowly but not too miserably. Maggie felt closer to her mother than she had done for years. Fay Tarrington put off her Bridge game and stayed at home, intent on providing sympathetic company. A new understanding was forged between them, and it warmed their embrace when Maggie took her leave on Sunday afternoon.

'Look after yourself, dear. You're the only daughter I've got,' her mother said tenderly.

'I'll be all right, Mum,' Maggie assured her, fighting down a well of feeling. 'It's only three days till Christmas. I'll be home on Wednesday night.'

Monday was a strain on her nerves, but the ordeal was lessened by the fact that she did not see Ian anywhere. Rhonda was agog at the news of the broken engagement, but she restrained her natural curiosity, warned off by Maggie's paleness and the tight look about the grey eyes. Bert dropped by to see her, but she brushed him off with a few over-bright pleasantries. It was a relief to get home to her apartment and be alone.

Common sense told her that each day would come easier. She made herself a scratch meal and settled in front of her television set, needing some light distraction to relax her. Nothing could be gained by letting her mind linger on what might have been. For the most part she sat there blankly, drifting in an emotional limbo, barely registering the shows being telecast.

The doorbell startled her, and she frowned and glanced at her watch. It was nine o'clock and she was not expecting anyone to call. Puzzled and a little apprehensive, she put the safety-chain on the lock before opening the door a small margin.

'It's all right, Maggie—it's me,' Pat Hollis said hurriedly. 'I know it's late, but I had to see you. May I come in?'

'Of course.' Maggie quickly slid the chain off, pulled the door wide and waved her in.

'Thanks,' Pat breathed, her eyes darting around the living-room as she entered. She swung back to Maggie who had not moved from the door. Her hands fluttered nervously. 'It's probably stupid of me . . . it sounds disloyal, but I had to talk to you about Ian. It's no good—I can't let it rest. I have to know!'

'Know what?' Maggie asked guardedly, and then remembered her manners. 'Sit down, Pat. Would you like a cup of coffee?'

'Thank you,' she nodded, sinking gratefully into a chair.

Maggie rushed into speech to cover the awkwardness of the moment. 'I'm sorry about last Friday night. I behaved very badly, what with having too much to drink and then getting weepy. It was very kind of you to bring me home.' She put the electric jug on to boil and reached down some clean mugs. Pat's silence was oppressive and Maggie chattered on. 'God knows what you must have thought of me! I don't usually carry on like that. I'm afraid I went a bit haywire. It was . . . it was a bad night for me.'

'Because your fiancé couldn't come?' Pat questioned hopefully.

Maggie turned from spooning instant coffee into the mugs and saw the anxiety in the large blue eyes. She did not know whether to lie or tell the truth. The jug boiled and the moment was postponed as she poured steaming water into the mugs, asking automatically about milk and sugar and adjusting the coffee to their liking. She carried in the mugs to a small occasional table and took the other armchair.

'You're not wearing your ring,' Pat observed tersely.

Maggie instinctively covered the bare finger, aware that it was too late as she did so. She flushed and picked up her mug of coffee to cover her agitation. 'No. I gave it back. That was why I was rather off-beam on Friday night. I'd decided that I couldn't keep . . . couldn't marry Dan,' she amended hastily.

'May I ask why? I know it's a terribly personal question, but . . . has it anything to do with Ian, Maggie?'

'Why should you think so?' Maggie said evasively. 'He knew about it. You must have seen him dancing with me. He asked me why I was so uptight and I'm afraid I blurted it out. I should never have got engaged to Dan in the first place. I let myself be persuaded into it.'

'Why?' Pat asked curiously. 'I mean, you either love someone or you don't.'

Maggie shrugged. 'The years were going past.

I'm twenty-five and not getting any younger. I guess every girl wants to get married and feel secure. My mother was pressuring me, Dan was pressuring me, and I gave in. It was always a mistake. Now it's over.'

Pat looked down at her hands and began playing with the solitaire diamond ring on her finger. Maggie recognised the action as one of deep uncertainty. Pat sucked in her breath as if to give her strength.

'What happened on Friday night, Maggie? I have to know! Please tell me.' Her gaze lifted and there was agony in those clear blue eyes. '. . . And tell me the truth.'

Maggie frowned, not knowing what to say and deeply conscious of the other girl's doubts.

'You see, what Ian says doesn't ring true, even though the words sound all right. I know you were deeply distressed. You'd been drinking recklessly and you cried all the way home. I was quite in sympathy with him seeing you safely to your apartment. But then Ian was so tense when he came back to the car. Did you ask him to stay, Maggie?'

'No!' The denial was emphatic. 'I was shocked when he . . . I mean, I didn't ask him, honestly.'

Pat looked searchingly at Maggie, her eyes puzzled. 'He said you needed him. That's what I don't understand. It . . . it suggests an intimacy between you. He swears it's not so, but . . . you're a beautiful woman, Maggie, clever, talented, a lot of things I'm not . . .'

'He loves you, Pat,' Maggie cut in sharply, unable to bear the wretchedness on the other girl's face. 'He doesn't love or even want me, if that's what you're asking. You're his woman.'

'That's what he says, but it doesn't answer, Maggie. There was . . . pain on his face on Friday night when he said you needed him. You don't feel pain for someone who means nothing to you.' Pat shook her head and her eyes were tired with disillusionment. 'You share his work, you're on the same intellectual level . . .'

'Don't, Pat! Don't put yourself down. You have qualities I don't possess. He does love you. There's nothing between Ian Drake and myself except perhaps a certain empathy. We share some similar feelings about things, that's all. He sensed how close I was to an emotional breakdown on Friday night and he held out a hand to stop it. He made me a cup of coffee and we talked for a while. Then he went home and I went to bed. I'm sorry you've been so upset by it.'

Pat nursed her mug of coffee, obviously mulling over the explanation. She drank some of it down and then replaced the mug on the table. 'Why did you say you were shocked? Didn't you let him in when he came back?'

'Pat, it doesn't matter,' Maggie began anxiously.

'I want to know. Can't you see I've got to know?' the other girl flared, and then simmered down, looking shamefaced. 'I'm sorry, you must think I'm a fool questioning you like this. I shouldn't expect you to answer. I don't know why I do, except that in spite of everything I like you. I admire you too. I can see that you and Ian would have a lot in common, more than he has with me. Please tell me what happened.'

Maggie sighed and rubbed her brow. It was a crazy situation. Here she was reassuring the woman so that Ian Drake could have what he wanted. It was not what Maggie wanted, but he had left her with no hope anyway. She looked across at her rival and resigned herself to the task.

'You're asking a lot, Pat, and I don't know that Ian Drake will thank me for it. You really have nothing to worry about. I was drunk. I knew I was going to be sick. When he unlocked my door for me I rushed past him to get to the bathroom. I slammed the door shut without even thinking of the key still being in it. I was hopelessly, wretchedly sick for quite a while. Then I sat on the bathroom floor and bawled my eyes out over the mess I'd made of my life.'

Maggie paused, not sure of how to go about explaining what happened next. Pat watched her with weighing eyes, demanding the truth.

'I can't remember how long I stayed there. I remember feeling too weak to move long after I stopped crying. I didn't know Ian was out here, holding a watching brief. I don't know what he thought—probably that I was carving myself up with razor blades. He came in to check on me and I made even more of a fool of myself because I was so shocked to see him there. He pushed me under the shower, then dragged me out and sobered me up. It wasn't a pretty scene. I'd say he was totally fed up with me by the time he left, but at least he'd straightened me out.'

'How did you feel? Did you want him to stay?'

A wave of hot colour swept up Maggie's cheeks. 'Pat,' she snapped angrily, 'you asked me what happened and I've told you the truth. He loves you. For God's sake, leave it alone. This leads nowhere.'

Pat shook her head. 'I love him, Maggie, but I always sensed that he held part of himself back. I was content with what I had until last Friday night. Now I'm not sure I'll be content. I'll have to think about it. You love him don't you?'

The blue eyes fixed on her with luminous clarity and Maggie could not dissemble. '*He* loves *you*,' she repeated hollowly.

'But he cares for you, Maggie. Maybe he doesn't realise how much. Maybe he's just being honourable, keeping to our engagement.'

Much as it hurt her to deny it, Maggie could not watch Pat's self-torture in silence. 'No, Pat. Believe me, he's not being honourable. You're the woman he wants.'

'I won't share him, Maggie,' Pat declared, lifting her chin proudly.

'He wouldn't expect you to.' A bitter smile twisted Maggie's mouth. 'Ian Drake controls his life. You should know that.' She stood up, unwilling to be catechised any further. 'I think I've told you all you have any right to know. Even if there was some kind of contest between us for Ian Drake's affections, you're the outright winner, so you can rest content. I'm not even in the running.'

Pat stood up, but she was not consoled. 'What happens next time you're in trouble, Maggie? Will he come to you? That's what I ask myself. It's a good question, isn't it?'

Maggie saw her out without another word. She knew instinctively that nothing good would come from this interview. If Pat Hollis showed her doubts to Ian Drake and revealed that she had visited Maggie, he would jump to the conclusion that Maggie had fed those doubts. She was in a no-win situation.

She could have told Pat about his kiss. She could have completely undermined Pat's faith in his love, wrecked their relationship, but it would only have earned Ian Drake's contempt. He had made his position too clear for Maggie to fool herself that there was any future with him for her.

She understood Pat's pain. If she was in the other girl's shoes, she would be suffering the same disillusionment. No matter how Ian Drake justified himself, he was cheating Pat. And he was cheating Maggie too. Pat had every right to resent the intimacy she sensed. Her intuition had not led her astray.

Maggie wandered off to bed. The problem was out of her hands. Her conscience was clear. Ian had confused the issue with his own ambivalent actions. She had not invited him into her apartment. It was up to him to reassure Pat. He had no grounds for accusing Maggie of making trouble.

She dropped into a restless sleep which made her feel even more ragged in the morning. There was little work to do at the office, just tying up a few loose ends, the tidying process which was the customary occupation this close to Christmas. There would be a rash of new jobs in the new year, business houses bringing out new products, but for the moment there was the lull before the holidays.

Peter Cameron had heard about her newly unattached state and came leering around, throwing out a few lines which Maggie studiously ignored.

'I suppose Bert Oliver's more to your liking,' he finally sneered when he got no rise to his baits.

'Why, Peter,' she smiled sweetly, 'how clever of you to guess! Do you think he'd go straight for me?'

He muttered something about her being as perverse as Bert and left her alone. She was still grinning to herself when Rhonda dropped by.

'Well, at least you're looking more cheerful. How goes it?'

'I'll survive,' Maggie assured her.

'Good for you. Doing anything special over Christmas?'

'No. Just spending it with Mum. You?'

Rhonda wrinkled her nose. 'Same old family get-together. But I like it,' she added with a grin. 'See you later.'

The day ended and Maggie gave herself an early night. She was too tired to do much else. She had tidied the apartment and packed a suitcase for tomorrow, intending to catch a train as soon as work finished. Travelling on Christmas Eve was never a picnic; the trains were always overcrowded with people intent on reaching families, and the later trains would be even more packed. She went to bed.

She had been in a deep sleep and only became slowly conscious of a shrill, insistent ringing. She struggled towards wakefulness, gradually realising it was the doorbell. She felt completely disorientated and literally staggered out to the door before her mind was active enough to question anything. She leaned against the door and focused on the digital wall-clock. One-thirty-eight. It was absurd for anyone to call at such a hour. She switched on the living-room light and looked at the safety-chain to check that it was on.

'Who's there?' she called out belligerently. The bell had stopped ringing when the light had switched on, but clearly someone was out there.

'Let me in, Maggie!'

It was Ian Drake's voice, harsh but distinctly his. Without giving it a second thought Maggie obeyed him.

# CHAPTER SIX

HE pushed the door shut behind him and leaned against it, his eyes examining Maggie with hard intensity. His silence and the bitter twist to his lips sent an apprehensive tingle up Maggie's spine. She was suddenly very conscious of the transparency of her thin cotton nightie and she pushed nervously at her tumbled hair, confused by his unexpected presence and embarrassed by the way he was looking at her.

'What are you doing here, Ian? Don't you know what time it is?' She fingered her nightie in agitation. 'You woke me out of a deep sleep.'

His gaze fell to her hand which was gathering folds of material in a subconscious attempt at modesty. Then slowly his eyes roved upwards, lingering on the rounded thrust of her breasts, the rapidly beating pulse in her throat, the soft perfection of her mouth, and at last, mockingly, he challenged the wide uncertainty of her eyes.

Then he moved, vaguely threatening as he closed in. He raised his hand to her cheek, caressing the fine skin around her eye with his thumb. 'Asleep, Maggie?' he murmured, a faintly mocking smile touching his lips. 'I didn't think of that. You see, I couldn't sleep at all. I kept thinking of you. I had this driving need to see you. You know about driving needs, Maggie.'

His hand suddenly thrust through her hair, pulling her roughly forward. The tone of his voice changed, deepening with a seething passion. 'I had this gnawing, empty feeling and I needed something to fill the emptiness. I thought about that and the answer was Maggie. Oh yes, I said to myself, Maggie would fill it. She wants to know what it feels like to be devoured.'

The last words were savagely grated out just before his mouth swooped on hers in a hard, punishing kiss. He gathered her in with one sweeping movement, pinning her against him. Maggie was so taken by surprise that she did not struggle. His mouth tasted of brandy and her first reaction was an instinctive revulsion to the intimacy he was forcing. Her brain was fogged by the sheer unexpectedness of his presence and the strange vehemence of his words.

Then abruptly the kiss changed, catching her off balance with its subtle persuasion, seducing her from her initial rejection and finally drawing a response. As soon as her surrender was complete he withdrew, breathing heavily.

'That's better, Maggie. That's what I want from you,' he muttered. 'Now, let's have it all.'

He picked her up in his arms, strode into the bedroom and dumped her unceremoniously on to the bed. He shrugged off his coat, then sat on the edge of the bed and began taking off his shoes and socks. Maggie drew her legs up, crouching near the pillow. She stared at him, totally confused by the emotion he had stirred and now the cool abruptness of his actions. The whole scene seemed unreal.

'What are you doing?' she asked stupidly.

'I'm getting undressed. What does it look as if I'm doing? Why don't you take off your nightie,

Maggie? Then I can have the pleasure of looking at that beautiful body of yours before I take it.'

He was discarding his shirt as he spoke and without hesitation he stood up to strip off his trousers.

'I don't understand. Why are you here?' Maggie gasped, her breathing accelerating at the sight of total masculinity, so carelessly revealed:

'I'm here to give you what you want. That's fair enough, isn't it? Do I have to undress you too?'

She resisted his first attempt to lift the nightie away, a surge of panic holding her rigid.

'Shall I tear it off? Does violence turn you on, Maggie?' he asked relentlessly.

'No,' she whispered, looking up at him with frightened eyes, knowing he was not speaking with the voice of love, yet not knowing what he could mean by coming to her like this.

'Then don't resist, because I'm not feeling particularly gentle at the moment.'

He whipped the nightie off and lifted her down on the bed, covering her body with his before she could voice a protest. Only then, with the shock of his nakedness crushing hers, did she begin to fight, pushing and clawing at him as he ravaged her mouth.

'No!' she choked out when his lips released hers.

'Isn't this what you wanted? What it was all for?' he grated out.

'No! Not like this, not like this,' she panted frantically, twisting and heaving to remove his weight, then beating at his shoulders when her efforts proved futile.

Ian dragged her hands away and kept them pinned above her head so that she was helpless. 'What did you expect?' he demanded cruelly.

'I didn't expect anything. Why should I?' Maggie was almost sobbing with fear. 'You told me you didn't want me. Let me go—oh, please, let me go!'

'But you want me, Maggie, and why should I be any less ruthless than you? You deliberately robbed me of the woman I wanted so that you could take her place. You owe me for that.'

'No, I didn't—I swear it! I've done nothing to hurt you. Nothing!'

'Pat broke our engagement tonight, and you were the reason, Maggie—you!' he continued relentlessly. 'Whatever you said to her, your words, your manner, whatever, there was no way I could change her mind back again. So here I am, all disengaged, and Pat informed me that you're disengaged too, so why are you fighting me? I'll give you what you want and take pleasure in doing it. You have a very desirable body.'

A shudder of revulsion ran through Maggie. 'Not that. Please, not that,' she pleaded brokenly. Tears were swimming out of the corners of her eyes and she rolled her head to one side, speaking in urgent gasps to keep him at bay. 'Pat came to me because of your actions, and I tried to explain them away. I did my best. I didn't tell her what happened. I knew you didn't want me—I told her so. It's not my fault. I'm sorry. I'm sorry. But it's not my fault. I didn't ask you in last Friday night, you know I didn't. And I didn't ask Pat to come last night. But I did my best for you, really

I did. I tried to clear her doubts. Don't do this to me—please, don't!'

A deep groan rumbled out of his throat and suddenly she was free. She instinctively curled into a protective ball and sobbed convulsively, all the misery and heartache of the last few days welling up in uncontrollable surges. For a long time she was unaware of the soft stroking on her naked back. It was only when her sobs degenerated into little shudders that the touch registered on her consciousness. Then she jerked away.

'It's all right, I won't hurt you. I'm sorry, Maggie.'

Ian sighed heavily and the bed creaked as he moved. Instantly she turned to face any danger, pressing herself against the wall to put distance between them. He was sitting on the edge of the bed, his body bent forward. Then he straightened and turned, holding her discarded nightie out to her. She snatched at it and hugged it across her breasts.

'It's all right,' he soothed. 'I'm not completely mad, just temporarily insane,' he added grimly. 'I didn't mean to be rough with you. I didn't come here to do that. I don't know why I came. I was drowning my sorrows in a bottle of brandy and suddenly I couldn't keep away. Then when I got here I couldn't keep my hands off you. I was driven beyond control, boiling with rage . . .'

'Because of Pat,' Maggie said dully, drained of emotion now that she had cried herself out.

He turned away, his head drooping forward as fingers raked through his hair. 'No. Pat was an excuse,' he muttered, and then drew in a sharp breath. 'I wanted you. I was angry at myself and angry at you. I keep telling myself . . .' He shook his head. 'I don't want to feel this way.'

'What way?' she asked softly, sensing that this was vitally important. A moment ago she had been numb, but now every nerve-end was electrified. She reached out and touched his shoulder, feeling the tension of hunched muscles. 'Tell me,' she whispered, coaxing him to reply.

He sighed. 'Best not to touch me, Maggie. I must go. You're all right now. Please forgive me for attacking you like that. The argument with Pat, the brandy, your . . . I was . . . off balance. Forgive me.' He dragged himself up as if it was an enormous effort of will.

'Don't go, Ian,' she whispered, frightened of what she was inviting but instinctively knowing that if he left now he would never come back again. This was his moment of weakness and she had to find out what he felt for her.

He half turned, hesitated, then stooped to pick up his clothes. 'I'll dress in your living-room and let myself out. Don't get up,' he rasped out, strain roughening his voice.

'Why are you turning your back on me?' she begged urgently. 'Why am I so undesirable to you?'

He paused, gripping the door-jamb as if to prevent himself from turning. The light from the living-room gleamed on the tight, corded muscles of his arms. She could see the rise and fall of his chest as he took a deep breath.

'Let me go, Maggie. I won't commit myself to you.'

Blind intuition voiced her reply. 'I'll never let you go. You're my other half.'

He swung around violently as if she had struck him. 'No! I'm me. I've fought too hard to be me. I won't be made dependent on anyone for anything.'

Maggie slid off the bed, her gaze never leaving his as she walked towards him, her hands outstretched in appeal. 'Not dependent, Ian. Partners. Sharing. You must feel it too, the same kinship I feel when I'm with you. It's too strong for it only to be on my side.'

'Stop there!' he commanded hoarsely. 'I warn you, Maggie!'

But the elation of power was dancing in her veins. All she had to do was reach out and claim him and he was hers. It was her only chance, and she took it, sliding her hands up the broad, muscular chest, watching the strain on his face which told all too clearly of the inward battle he was fighting. Then victory was hers. His arms enclosed her with savage strength, moulding her to his body as he rained feverish kisses on her face and hair.

'I told you. Damn you, Maggie! You're a witch, stealing my soul. One night and no more—do you hear me? Is that what you want? Will you be satisfied with that?'

'No,' she breathed, ecstatically turning her face for the fervent worship of his lips.

'You've got to be. You've got to be. I can't let you win,' he muttered, but Maggie wasn't listening any more. He took her mouth in a long, searing kiss which ignited all the repressed passion in their blood. 'Maggie,' he breathed like a prayer in her ear as he cradled her against him, twining her hair through his fingers. 'I've got to have you, just this once . . . maybe it'll set me free of this . . . this torment. Oh God, how I need you!'

Then he was lifting her and they were back on the bed and he was kissing her eyelids shut, oh, so gently, and the caress of his hands was like magic on her skin and his body was hers to hold and touch and explore in a slow, pagan ritual of sensuality which he led and encouraged by example. Maggie was intoxicated with wave after wave of sweet, aching pleasure as his lips and tongue roved freely. Her breasts tingled with swollen excitement, her legs quivered with exquisite anticipation, and finally, when their need was at fever-pitch, Ian thrust for total possession. Maggie gasped at the brief, tearing pain, but when he hesitated her hands reassured him, urging him to go on, her body arching to his because nothing could now stop the compulsion which drove them both towards the final, necessary fulfilment.

She clutched at him, possessing his body as urgently as he was possessing hers, moaning with the need to reach whatever had to be reached. Then suddenly they were there, and the explosion of pleasure was so glorious she felt she was sinking through layers and layers of melting warmth, and he kissed her once again, softly this time, her body hummed with a new harmony, and it was complete.

They lay in silence, his head on the pillow next to hers, their breaths intermingling, hearts slowly returning to normal pace. Maggie stroked his smooth, muscular body in soft wonderment, believing in that moment that it would always be hers to touch, feel, hold in her arms and know it as she knew it now. She turned her face to his and whispered, 'I love you.'

Ian sighed and ran his hand gently over her soft, warm contours. 'That wasn't love, Maggie. It was possession. Don't give it any other name. Why didn't you tell me you were a virgin?'

'I love you,' she repeated, giving him the only answer she had.

He shook his head restlessly. 'You burden me with that too. I didn't want to be your first lover. I thought . . . Oh, hell and damnation! What am I to do with you?' he demanded with a touch of desperation.

'Love me,' she whispered, kissing the corners of his mouth and snuggling closer, hugging him to her.

He stroked her hair as he spoke with dry mockery. 'Love is a trap. You get sucked in by all the shining promises of love and you grow dependent, thinking love will last for ever. Then it disappears and you're left crippled because you've given too much of yourself away. Don't put love on me, Maggie. I won't wear it.'

'You said you loved Pat,' she reasoned tentatively, wary of bringing her name up even now.

His silence was heavy with brooding. At last he said haltingly, 'Pat . . . suited me. I could have lived happily with her . . . not with you, Maggie. You're a nightmare.'

She stiffened and a horrible stillness grew inside her. 'What do you mean?' she asked, because the question had to be asked. She had to know.

'There's no peace of mind with you.'

'Why not?'

'Why not, she asks!' and the words had a mocking lilt. 'You lie there like Circe, singing your insidious song of love, weaving a spell of enchantment designed to make me forget everything but you. If I give in my whole life means nothing. I will have betrayed myself, and I'd hate that, Maggie, and eventually I'd hate you.' He sighed and resettled himself, one hand behind his head, the other playing with her hair in a desultory fashion. 'It would be so easy to give in. You're a witch, a beautiful, black-haired witch, giving me your virginity like a sacrificial offering that will bind me to you. That wasn't fair, Maggie, and I won't accept responsibility for it. This was your doing, your choice.'

'You came to me,' she reminded him, a tight ball of fear in her stomach.

'Like a drug addict hungering for a fix,' he agreed dryly. 'And at this moment I want nothing else but to lose myself in the magic you cast, but it's all a dream, an infinitely desirable dream, and I'd like to believe in it, but there's always tomorrow and I have to wake up.'

'No. It's real, Ian, what we have together. Don't let it go. Don't let me go. I need you,' she begged, pressing her lips to his to stop the destructive flow of words.

She felt the rise of passion in him and fed it with her own until he groaned with the same primitive need which fired her. There was no gentleness this time, but she exulted in the wildness of his lovemaking. When she gasped for breath he stole it again, driving her crazy with his passionate onslaught. She was a heaving mass of chaotic emotion when he took her, and the intense pleasure was almost pain, fiercely demanding to be assuaged.

Possession was almost frantic, a keen sense of desperation communicating itself as they climbed faster and higher, urgently reaching for that necessary plateau where they could be at peace. It burst upon them like a kaleidoscope of brilliant colour, revolving through their bodies in ripples of light, releasing the dark, imprisoning tension with a multitude of hues, bathing them both in blissful contentment. Their bodies remained locked together lest the light might fade away at any movement and their oneness was a beautiful thing, complete in every way. After a long, long silence, Ian stirred. Maggie clung to him possessively.

'Don't go!'

He nuzzled the curve of her throat and shoulder. 'How can I?' he breathed raggedly, clinging to her with equal possession, and she took his words as surrender.

She relaxed, warm and secure in his arms, and gradually sleep claimed her. It was a heavy, dreamless sleep and subconsciously she resented the touch on her face which was demanding she wake up. Her hand reached up to brush it away, but her fingers encountered other fingers which curled around hers.

'Wake up, Maggie.'

Ian's murmur held a determined note which jangled warningly in her ears. Her eyelids flew open and he was sitting there on the side of her bed, fully dressed, neat, tidy, even clean-shaven, very much ready to leave. Her hand gripped his with sudden panic.

'No,' she whispered as her eyes saw the withdrawal in his, the grave lines of his face and the grim set to his mouth.

'I have to go, Maggie. I couldn't leave without . . . some acknowledgement. I did tell you. I can't accept . . . I don't know whether to thank you or curse you for last night . . . I can't exist in you. I have to be free. Please try to understand.'

His eyes were dark with turmoil, yet they pleaded for her to release him, and the pain of loss began its monstrous growth in Maggie's heart. She did not understand at all. He was leaving her, but surely it could not be a final leavetaking, not after what they had shared last night.

'You don't mean . . . you can't mean . . . you'll come back to me sometimes,' she begged, her voice quivering between hope and despair.

He closed his eyes and shook his head. 'No. That wouldn't be fair on you.' His eyelids lifted reluctantly and there was all the bleakness of rejection in his gaze. 'It would torment us both. You'll find someone, someone else who'll answer your needs.' He drew his hand out of hers and rose to his feet. 'Goodbye, Maggie.'

'I'll see you at work, Ian. What then?' she cried in desperate appeal.

He had already turned away from her and he only glanced back fleetingly. 'Nothing then. That's inescapable but impersonal. Impersonal, Maggie. Don't make it anything else.'

She nodded sadly. 'That's it, then. You're going.' The words were flat and unemotional because if she let go her control she would storm at him, raging against his decision in a torrent of emotion which would only humiliate her further and she had nothing left but a little scrap of pride.

He moved stiffly, as if he had to concentrate hard to keep going, but he did not turn back again nor say another word.

She thought she had felt empty when she had broken her engagement to Dan, but now she was whirling down an endless dark void and there was pain, a terrible, wrenching pain that billowed through her body, torturing her with the magnitude of her loss. She had gambled and lost. She had given herself totally, unable to believe that her gift could be rejected, and it had been so right, so completely perfect, that now the memory of their union was the greatest pain of all because it would never be repeated.

She slid her hand down her naked body trying to recapture the warmth, but she was cold and her skin did not tingle with life. It shivered with rejection. She dragged the blankets around her and lay there completely still, absorbing the pain in blank helplessness. She had lost and the loss would echo on, all through her life, because there would be no one else. Perfection could not be repeated, and Maggie was a perfectionist who could not accept less.

# CHAPTER SEVEN

SHE did not go in to the office. When she finally dragged herself out of the mire of despair it was too late to bother, and she had no inclination to mouth expressions of goodwill for Christmas when her own spirits were at rock bottom. For a long time she sat staring at her packed suitcase, wondering if she could stand going home to Wallareen, knowing that her mother would be anxiously cheerful and overly watchful of Maggie's mood. In the end she decided that Christmas was Christmas and she owed it to her mother to go home.

Fay Tarrington welcomed her, but Maggie had encased herself in a shell of reserve and found it difficult to respond. There were invitations to various social activities, but Maggie politely declined them all. Her mother's friends dropped by to toast the season in a number of convivial drinks. Their manner to Maggie was one of gentle sympathy, as if she was the delicate sufferer of the broken engagement. The irony of it wryly amused her, but she answered their questions with careful vagueness.

Dan telephoned twice, but Maggie refused to take the calls. He arrived at the house late in the afternoon of Christmas day. Maggie shut herself in her bedroom, not emerging until her mother insisted that he had given up and gone away and dinner would be ruined if she did not come down and eat it. Fay Tarrington waited until her daughter was seated at the table before delivering a comment.

'He loves you, Maggie. Why won't you at least talk to him?' she urged with soft persuasion.

'There's nothing to talk about. Everything's been said,' Maggie stated with determined finality. Dan was far, far in the past, almost blotted out by the all-pervasive image of Ian Drake.

'Listen to me, dear. You said yourself that there's no chance of your marrying this other man. At least Dan . . .'

'No, it's over. Dead. Don't try raking over the ashes, Mum.'

There was a tense silence until Fay Tarrington sighed and began speaking about the night's television programmes. Dan's name was not mentioned again. Maggie was a little ashamed of her impatient outburst, but she did not regret it.

For the last two days Maggie had felt beaten by Ian's rejection of her love, but rebellion was now stirring in her heart. She was going to fight that decision of his. The memory of their lovemaking gave her the spur for action. He had been as much involved as she that night and nothing he had said afterwards could dim that certainty in her mind. Whatever his reasons for turning his back on her, they could not be as important as sharing the kind of love which was possible between them.

She did not believe that he could carry out his intention to be impersonal when he saw her. He had been unable to be impersonal ever since that day in the taxi after they had lunched with the

Jamieson people. The strength of the attraction between them was too great and the emotional bond would only have been strengthened by what they had experienced together. She loved him, she wanted him, and she intended to win him back to her side.

'I'm not sure I'll be coming home for New Year, Mum,' she said as she was leaving to catch the train back into the city on Sunday afternoon. 'I'll ring you and let you know. Okay?'

Her mother frowned. 'I don't like to think of you brooding alone in your apartment.'

'I won't brood, Mum—that's a promise. I've got things to do,' Maggie retorted on a cheerful note.

Fay Tarrington brightened. 'That's all right, then, but do let me know.'

And I don't intend to be alone either, Maggie added privately, knowing that her mother would be shocked at her daughter's plans.

There was nothing she could do until tomorrow, because Maggie did not know Ian's home address. The telephone directory listed several Drake I.'s, but she did not feel inclined to wade through wrong numbers on the offchance of reaching him. He might very well have an unlisted number. Besides, it was better to see him face to face. She needed every advantage. Ian was too strong a man to bend easily.

Her plans to arrange a meeting received a sharp setback on Monday morning. Jane Carfield informed her that Mr Drake was not expected back at the office until Wednesday morning and he had left strict instructions not to make any appointments for him on that day. Maggie was tempted to ask for Ian's private number, but knew the request would only draw a sniff of disapproval from the officious secretary.

Disappointed but undeterred in her quest, Maggie spent a half-hour on Monday night telephoning all the Drake I.'s. She drew a red circle around the number which did not answer. All the rest had been accounted for. Anxious to reach him before the New Year weekend, she dialled the circled number several times on Tuesday night, but there was still no answer. On the final try, Ian's voice came over the line, identifying himself in a peremptory fashion. Maggie cut the connection without a word.

She showered and changed into a blue cotton sundress which was sexy without being obviously so. The bodice fitted her like a glove and it was buttoned through to the hem of the flared skirt. She quickly applied a little eye make-up and some fresh lipstick, brushed her hair, slipped on some high-heeled sandals, and with her pulse dancing an excited little jig she telephoned for a taxi.

Having given the taxi-driver Ian's address Maggie sat back in the cab and tried to order her thoughts. A lot would depend on Ian's susceptibility to her, but she had to anticipate that his first reaction to her visit would be negative. Somehow she would have to persuade him to at least talk to her. That was the first step. The taxi-ride was short, barely ten minutes, and would have been shorter if the driver had been familiar with the narrow one-way streets. Woolhara Mansions was the address, just into the next suburb to Paddington where Maggie had her apartment. She stepped out of the cab and paid the driver.

The building was in fact a large, old-style brick
mansion, heavily ornate with the wrought-iron
lacework of its period. Since Ian's address was
listed as Apartment 2 it had obviously been
divided into self-contained units. She opened the
spiky wrought-iron gate and let it clang shut
behind her. The short path ended in wide steps
leading up to the glass-panelled front doors of
the house. The doors were shut but not locked.
Maggie entered the spacious foyer and with a
sigh of relief she found the first door on her left
numbered 2. She pressed the bell before courage
deserted her. She waited, nerves on edge, her
heart pounding its protest against the tight
constriction in her chest.

The door opened and Ian stared at her blankly,
his face etched in lines of fatigue. He lifted a
hand and dragged it down his face as if wiping off
a daze. Then he looked at her again. 'What are
you doing here, Maggie?' he asked wearily.

'I had to see you, Ian.' Her voice came out in a
husky whisper and she hastily swallowed to
moisten her throat. 'May I come in?'

He held on to the door and leaned his other
arm against the jamb, effectively blocking any
entry. He bowed his head and drew in a deep
breath before lifting it again. His eyes were hard
coals of darkness. 'I don't want to see you. I
thought I made that clear, Maggie,' he said with
soft deadliness.

'No, it wasn't clear,' she replied quickly.
'Nothing is very clear at all and I'd like to talk
about it. Please. I think you owe me that,' she
added desperately.

He shook his head. 'No. I don't owe you

anything, and I won't submit to emotional blackmail.'

'Then just out of plain decency or common courtesy, ask me in, Ian, because I have something to say to you.'

It seemed an agonising length of time before he nodded. 'All right, come in.'

He showed her into a large, tall-ceilinged room. Bookcases flanked a marble fireplace and a workmanlike desk was in one corner. The polished parquet flooring was scattered with thick rugs and three loose-cushioned sofas were grouped around the hearth for conversation and relaxation. There was a homely, lived-in atmosphere about the room, but Maggie was too tense to enjoy it. Ian waved her to sit down.

'Would you like a drink?' he asked with formal politeness.

'No . . . yes, I would, thank you. A dry sherry if you have one.'

She had not eaten and the sherry might untie some of the knots in her stomach. A half-filled whisky glass stood on a low table and a turned-down magazine indicated where Ian had been sitting when interrupted. She took the opposite seat and watched him pour sherry from a cut-glass decanter. He was casually dressed in jeans and T-shirt, but he did not look relaxed. He gripped the decanter tightly. Then his hand enclosed the small glass as he carried it over and placed it on the table in front of her. Having resumed his own seat he leaned back with his arms folded, observing her guardedly.

'The other night was a mistake, Maggie, and I don't intend to repeat it. I don't want you complicating my life, distorting the shape I've chosen to make of it. I don't think I can speak more clearly than that,' he stated with cool precision.

She flushed and took a slow sip of sherry to give herself a moment to control her emotions. 'Would you tell me why it was a mistake?' she asked as calmly as she could. 'I thought it was something very special.'

'That doesn't alter anything,' he said with slow vehemence, almost grating out the words. 'But yes, it was special. Let it stay that way. Don't drag it on, Maggie, please. I don't want to hurt you . . .'

'You know you are by rejecting me like this,' she cut in urgently. 'Will you tell me why you're doing it? I just don't understand, Ian. We could have something so good . . .'

'No!' The harsh negative whipped off his tongue as he jack-knifed forward. His hand snatched up the glass of whisky, but he did not drink it. He leaned his elbows on his knees and nursed the glass in his hands, brooding over it. 'I don't want what you're offering. I don't want it, Maggie, so leave me alone. I wish I'd never met you.' He raised eyes which burned with resentment. 'I wish I'd never met you,' he repeated savagely.

'Why? What have I done?' she pleaded, frantic to understand his reasoning.

He hooded his eyes and sighed. 'Nothing. You . . . are you. The interaction between us . . . happened, that's all. It wasn't your fault. I'm sorry it happened. I didn't plan for it, and it got out of hand. Now it's over.'

'Is it, Ian? Can you honestly say that?' Maggie demanded bitterly.

He looked up and met her accusation head on. 'No, it's not over, but it will be, Maggie, because I'm working on it, and when I concentrate hard on something I always succeed. Please accept what I'm telling you. I've been polite. Now I want to you to finish your drink and go, because staying here will not accomplish anything but nervous wear on both of us.'

Maggie's hand was shaking as she replaced the glass of sherry on the table. 'I don't want it after all,' she murmured huskily, blinking back the tears that threatened. She could not keep beating her head against the brick wall of his resistance. She stood up with as much dignity as she could manage and started to follow him to the door.

Her vision was blurred and her high heel caught in one of the rugs. She stumbled and Ian automatically turned back to grab her arm. Maggie staggered against his broad chest and for one tempting moment she let her palms linger there, feeling the taut muscles and the sharp intake of his breath. She glanced up and saw the torment of desire in his eyes. Instinctively she pressed closer, her hands slipping upwards to curl around his neck.

'No!' The word wrenched out of him through gritted teeth. His hands reached up and tore hers away, holding them tightly at her sides. 'Not again, Maggie,' he breathed heavily. 'I won't let you do this to me. I'm my own man.'

'But I love you,' she whispered from the aching depths of her heart.

It was the wrong thing to say. His control

snapped. A fierce hatred leapt out of his eyes and he spat the word out. 'Love! Don't talk to me of love!' He dropped her hands as though they were unclean and stepped away from her. 'The last thing I need is love,' he said contemptuously, his hands making a sharp, cutting gesture. 'Go and give your love to someone else. Barlow! Didn't he want it? Go back to him and leave me free of your love. It's a snare, a killing snare, and I won't be caught up in it—never again! Go on, go!'

She stood there, too stunned to move. He turned his back on her in rigid disgust. Then he wheeled around angrily, shooting out his fist in defiance. 'I'd take Pat back if she'd have me. You and I were better off before we ever met. I don't want you and your love. Do you hear me?' he shouted in hoarse rage.

'Yes, I hear you,' she whispered.

From somewhere she dredged up the strength to move. Her legs were trembling, but she walked away from him. She found herself out on the footpath with no recollection of having left the house, but she kept walking, putting one foot in front of the other. Eventually she reached a well-lit street of shops and there were buses and other traffic cruising along the road. She stopped and forced herself to take some bearings. A vacant taxi loomed up and she flagged it down.

Once back in her apartment she picked up the telephone and dialled. Her mother answered the summons on the third ring. 'Hello, Mum. I'm coming home,' Maggie said dully.

'I'm glad you changed your mind, dear. I'll see you tomorrow night, then.'

'No, I'll catch the morning train. I'll take tomorrow off.'

'Did your plans fall through? I thought you said you had things to do.'

'No, there's nothing. Nothing at all. I'm coming home.'

Maggie hung up and walked into her bedroom. She undressed and went to bed. For a long time she lay awake staring into the darkness, seeing nothing, nothing at all.

The next day she got up, packed a case and went home to Wallareen. She chatted to her mother for a while, ate a token lunch, then picked up a book and settled herself in the lounge-room to read. Her mind did not grasp the thread of the story, but her eyes moved over the words and she kept turning pages. After dinner she sat watching television with her mother. When the doorbell rang it was Fay Tarrington who rose to answer it. Maggie was not even aware of her mother leaving the room.

'Maggie?'

Dan's voice drifted through the fog in her mind. He was taking her mother's chair, drawing it closer to hers, sitting down, smiling his charming smile.

'Hello, Dan,' she said automatically.

'Now you don't have to worry that I'll start pressuring you,' he said quickly, spreading his hands in a conciliatory manner. 'You don't want to marry me and I accept that, but that doesn't make us enemies, does it, Maggie? Surely we can be civilised friends.'

'If that's what you want,' she agreed carelessly.

'Well, in that case, I think it'd be a friendly

thing if you'd come with me to the Wilcoxes' party tonight,' he continued smoothly. 'We were invited, you know, and after all, it is New Year's Eve.' He held up his hands to forestall any protest. 'No pressure, Maggie. Just a bit of fun and relaxation. You like Claire and Trevor. Why shouldn't you come and enjoy their party? Our broken engagement shouldn't stop you. I'll simply be your escort for the night. How's that?'

He smiled an open, friendly smile. Maggie stared at him, her face blank of expression. Words were echoing through her mind. 'Go and give your love to someone else. Barlow. Didn't he want it? Go back to him.'

'All right, Dan. Why not?' she said abruptly, rising to her feet immediately. 'I'll go and change.'

His surprise at such an easy victory was written all over his face, but Maggie did not wait for any comment from him. She headed straight upstairs, picked up a bathrobe from her bedroom and went to have a quick shower. Afterwards she took her time making up her face. There was no hurry. Dan would wait. The eyeshadow and mascara could not hide the lifelessness of her eyes, but they helped to put superficial life into her pale face. She brushed her hair and then shrugged off the bathrobe ready to dress.

Her naked body was reflected in the mirror and she paused to look at it, objectively noting the high, full breasts, slender waist, the sweeping curve of hip and thigh. There was nothing wrong with her body. Most girls would envy the perfect contours, but not even her desirable body had been able to sway Ian from his decision. He did not want her.

She turned away, took the red crêpe dress from her wardrobe and slipped it on. A pair of pantyhose was drawn on, her feet slipped into elegant shoes, and she was ready. Maggie did not question what she was doing. She walked down the stairs with her back straight and her head held high. Dan was in the sitting-room conversing with her mother. Maggie paused in the doorway.

'I'm ready,' she announced bluntly.

His grin was all pleasure as his eyes ran over her. There was pleasure on her mother's face too, but Maggie could not find a smile within herself. Dan said goodnight to her mother, took Maggie's arm and escorted her to his car, stringing together a lot of breezy comments as they walked. She barely heard them. He chatted on as he drove, giving a detailed account of a party he had attended on Boxing Day. He did not remark on her silence until they pulled up outside the Wilcox house. Then he reached over and gently squeezed her hand.

'Maggie, if you'd prefer not to go in to the party, that's all right by me. Just say what you want.'

She glanced down at the hand holding hers and then up at him. 'I don't mind going in, Dan.'

He frowned. 'You're sure? I thought you might not want a crowd of people. You seem kind of closed in upon yourself.'

'Maybe I need a party to brighten me up.'

He scanned her face thoughtfully and then nodded.

The party was noisy, all the guests exuberant with the kind of mad spirits that New Year's Eve always evoked. The hi-fi blared out lively music.

Maggie was soundly kissed by several male acquaintances and pressed into dancing. Dan did not attempt to be in any way possessive. He saw that she always had company and supplied her with food and drinks. A few people remarked on their broken engagement, but Maggie and Dan ignored the questions and innuendoes and the topic was dropped. The constant noise seemed to throb through Maggie's head, echoing through all the empty places, and the pounding grew worse as the night wore on. Claire Wilcox noticed her holding her forehead and made a sympathetic grimace.

'Headache, Maggie? Why don't you have a quiet lie down in our room for a while? You can't leave the party before midnight.'

'Thanks, Claire, I might do that.'

'It's just down the hallway and to your right. I'll tell Dan where you've gone, and he can come and get you before the whistles start blowing. Okay?'

Maggie nodded and slipped away from the crowd. The bedroom door shut off most of the noise and she crawled on to the bed and sank her head into a cool pillow. She just lay still, unaware of time passing, and yet it did not seem long before Dan came in, quietly closing the door behind him.

'Maggie? Are you awake?' he whispered.

'Yes.'

He came and sat on the edge of the bed and gently caressed the hair away from her temples. 'Headache bad?'

'Yes.'

'Turn over and I'll give you a neck massage. It'll release any tension.'

She did not resist nor make any protest when he rolled her over and undid the halter tie of her dress. He lifted her hair aside and his hands began their massage around her neck and shoulders. It felt good. She lay there passively accepting his ministrations, her mind empty of all thought. The pain in her head seemed to ease away. Slowly she became aware that the massage was no longer a massage but a caress and Dan's hands were stroking her, down the curve of her spine and all over her naked back. Then he gently turned her over and the halter top of her dress slipped aside. She automatically reached up to fix it in place again, but Dan stopped her hand. He pulled down the bodice and looked at her.

His fingers trailed lightly over the soft swell of her breasts and Maggie made no move to stop him. She lay perfectly still, waiting. His thumb teased her nipples erect and he bent to kiss them with a slow sensuality which should have aroused some desire in her. His lips grazed over her skin and still she felt nothing. His mouth reached hers and she opened her lips, giving him the intimacy he sought without resistance. As an experiment it was an abject failure. Dan was breathing heavily when he withdrew. He lifted her enough to hold her in a close embrace, her breasts crushed against the soft silk of his shirt. His fingers thrust through her hair, pressing her head closer to his.

'I want you, Maggie,' he breathed into her ear.

The words were seductive. Ian did not want her. It was nice to be wanted.

'Come home with me now,' Dan whispered.

'I'll take care of you, darling. I'll love you as you should be loved.'

Love. Love with a stranger. Dan was a stranger, and she could not give him her love. She only wanted Ian, Ian's hands on her, his body possessing hers, his mouth . . . She struggled out of Dan's embrace and pushed herself away. 'No, it wouldn't be right. It wouldn't work,' she told him despairingly. Her hands fumbled with her dress, finding the ends of her halter top and fastening them around her neck.

Dan stood and pulled her to her feet. His hands slid down to her hips, thrusting her against him, making her aware of his arousal. 'Why didn't you stop me?' he demanded angrily. 'You let me touch you, kiss you. Why the hell didn't you stop me if it wasn't what you wanted?'

'Because I hoped it would work, but it didn't,' she answered with painful honesty. 'I don't love you, Dan. I'm sorry for letting you go on, but if it went any further I'd really be cheating you.'

'I don't care if you think you're cheating me. I want you, Maggie—I've wanted you from the moment I first set eyes on you. Let me make love to you. I swear I'll make you happy,' he pleaded feverishly.

Her heart cringed at the thought of anyone but Ian making love to her. 'I can't. I'm sorry, Dan, but I can't. Please let go of me. I'll call for a taxi. I shouldn't have come with you—it was wrong. I can only hurt you. Don't call on me again, Dan, Put me out of your mind. I'm no good to you.'

She pushed away from him and whirled out of the room before he could stop her. The numbness which had fogged her brain was gone now, and she could think clearly again. Ian did not want her and sooner or later she had to come to terms with that fact, but it did not excuse her for hurting someone else. She could not use others to blanket the inner core of pain. Her passage to the telephone was interrupted by various people, and Dan intercepted her before she could make the call.

'I'll take you home, Maggie,' he said determinedly. 'I brought you and I'll take you home.' He drew a deep breath and added, 'I apologise for pressuring you, but you'd have to admit you did hand me the temptation. Now just let me take you home.'

Maggie scanned his face anxiously. She did not want to add insult to injury and he seemed to be under control. 'All right, if you wish,' she agreed unsteadily.

They took their leave of their hostess with a minimum of fuss, Dan explaining that Magie's headache was worse and he was taking her home. Claire Wilcox gave them an arch look as if she knew better, but Dan did drive Maggie straight home and conscientiously escorted her to the front door.

'I hope you feel better tomorrow. Goodnight, Maggie,' he said calmly, giving her elbow a light squeeze.

'Make it goodbye, Dan, and thank you for bringing me home.'

He shook his head. 'Not goodbye. We're friends, aren't we?'

'No, I don't think we can be friends. It's goodbye, Dan. I meant what I said earlier. Accept it. I have to,' she sighed.

'Have you any idea how I feel?' he retorted tightly.

She looked up at him with bleakly resigned eyes. 'Yes, I know how it feels. Goodbye, Dan.'

Before he could say any more she opened the door and slipped inside, closing it firmly behind her. The light was still on in the sitting-room and there was the sound of exploding fireworks from the television. The old year had ended, along with a lot of other things, Maggie thought sadly. A whole new year stretched ahead of her, empty, unmarked, waiting to be filled. And she would fill it somehow. Losing Ian was not quite the end of the world. Not quite, she repeated grimly to herself, and went in to join her mother.

# CHAPTER EIGHT

'HELLO, Maggie.'

The voice held a jarring note. Maggie reluctantly dragged her gaze up from the shoe she had been examining and looked into the speculative blue eyes of Pat Hollis. Caught off guard, Maggie simply stared for a moment. Then a flush of embarrassment crawled up her neck and she found her tongue.

'Hello, Pat. Are you looking for bargains too?'

The January sales were on in all the big department stores and the two girls faced each other across a display table of shoes, all marked down to half price.

'Yes, but I don't know why I bother looking at shoes. The sizes are always too large or too small.'

'I have the same problem. Sometimes I wish I didn't have average feet.'

'Well, there's not much else average about you, Maggie,' Pat remarked dryly. 'How's Ian these days?'

The acid little note in Pat's voice brought a twist of irony to Maggie's lips. 'I presume he's well. I haven't heard anything to the contrary.'

The blue eyes mocked her. 'Look, you don't have to pull your punches now. It's all over between me and Ian and I know how he feels about you. I can't imagine you've wasted any time getting together.'

Pain savaged Maggie's heart for a moment and she idly picked up a shoe, pretending to examine it while she fixed her composure. 'I haven't laid eyes on Ian since before New Year.' She glanced back at Pat and saw the disbelief in her eyes change to puzzlement.

'Have you been away on holiday or something?'

Maggie sighed and gave a wry smile. 'No, I've been working as usual. I don't work near the executive offices, you know. I'm on a different floor altogether in my own little cubicle,' she added in explanation. 'Ian is the boss. I'm merely an employee and we don't mix except when business demands it.'

The disbelief was back in Pat's eyes. 'Come on, Maggie, who are you trying to kid? I may not be as bright as you, but I'm far from stupid. You broke your engagement because of Ian and now that he's free of me, what's to stop either of you? I know he wants you.'

'No, I told you he didn't want me, Pat. You should have believed me,' Maggie said wearily. 'It probably would have been better for all of us if you had.'

'But Maggie, I talked to Ian on New Year's Day.' Pat paused and sucked in a deep breath before grabbing Maggie's arm. 'Look, we've got to talk. Come and have a coffee with me. This doesn't make sense.'

'What doesn't make sense?'

'Come on, I could do with resting my feet for a bit anyway.'

Maggie let herself be drawn along, curious in spite of her reservations about discussing Ian. Pat steered her to a vacant table in the corner of the cafeteria and almost pushed her into a chair.

'I'll get the coffees. I owe you one anyway,' she declared, and hurried off before Maggie could argue.

The situation had been thrust upon her, so Maggie resigned herself to listening and tried to relax. Pat soon returned and settled herself with an air of determination.

'You know I broke my engagement to Ian,' she began.

'Yes, I know,' Maggie replied quietly, her attention fixed on the spoon stirring sugar into her coffee.

'He didn't want it broken. He argued and argued, but I wouldn't listen. I was in a ferment about you and I wouldn't listen. I felt hurt and I was really lashing back at him because he'd stayed with you that night instead of coming home with me. Anyhow, after a few days I thought it over and decided I'd been a fool, so I went to him on New Year's Day, meaning to apologise and accept him again. Only he'd changed his mind. He said it was too late. He was sorry that he'd hurt me, but it was too late to mend our engagement. He looked tormented, the same as when he went back to you after the office party. I asked him straight out was it because of you, and he said . . .'

Pat frowned and hesitated and Maggie held her breath, scared yet fascinated in a compulsive need to know it all.

'He said, "Maggie doesn't own me." He said it so savagely as if . . . oh, I don't know. He became very tense and angry when I spoke of you and I didn't know what to think. I swallowed my pride and asked him for a second chance. He covered his face with his hands and I waited, and then he said he was sorry, but I'd been right about you, that you got in the way. It was no use contemplating a renewal of our engagement because you'd always lie between us. It was a complete switch-about from having denied you only a week before, but I had to believe him. The truth was there on his face. Yet now you say he hasn't even seen you. It doesn't make sense!'

Incredulity echoed in Pat's voice, but her story only gave Maggie the satisfaction of knowing that Ian could no more follow his claim of accepting Pat back, than she could follow his advice to return to Dan.

'Does it make any sense to you?' Pat asked persistently.

'Perhaps he wants to be free.'

Pat shook her head. 'I don't get it.'

Maggie sighed. 'No, I don't know that I do either, but he doesn't want me and that's that.'

'Well, he doesn't want me either,' Pat said glumly.

'I guess we'd better both just look for someone else,' Maggie suggested by way of commiseration. 'Anyone on your horizon?'

'One possible,' Pat said with a wry grin. 'He's not another Ian Drake, but he's nice, and he's more my level, if you know what I mean. Unfortunately millionaires are few.'

'Is Ian a millionaire? I wouldn't have thought . . .'

'Maybe not, but he's awfully rich and

successful, and all from nothing. Did you know he was brought up in a welfare institution?'

'An orphan?' Maggie asked in surprise, thinking how strange it was that she could have been intimate with a man and yet know nothing of his background. He had just been Ian, the one man who could bring her really alive.

'Not exactly. A deserted child, I think. He always glossed over his childhood, though he said he didn't mind being in an institution.'

Deserted. The word rolled around Maggie's brain like a drum, pounding out its message of import. Ian had been a deserted child. Had that embittered him towards love? And yet if he had never known his mother . . . 'How old was he?' she blurted out.

'What?'

'How old was Ian when he was deserted?'

Pat frowned and shrugged her ignorance on the point. 'I don't know. Though, come to think of it, it couldn't have been as a baby, unless . . . oh, I don't know. Maybe he had foster-parents. I think he was only in the orphanage from about age eight or nine. That's only an impression. He was never specific about it. Why do you want to know?'

Eight or nine. An impressionable age. Old enough to suffer from rejection. Young enough never to forgive it.

'Maggie?'

She looked vaguely at Pat, her mind totally concentrated on the implications of that childhood desertion. 'You say he stayed in a welfare institution from then on . . . all the time through his adolescence.'

Pat was puzzled by Maggie's persistence on the subject, but she answered goodnaturedly. 'I guess so. I did ask once if he wasn't invited out, you know, by families for Christmas or something. You hear about such things being organised for kids in orphanages. He said he didn't choose to go.'

He didn't choose. Yes, the damage went back to then. He didn't choose. Ian had loved his mother or foster-mother and she had deserted him, handed him in like an unwanted package. It had to have been such a traumatic shock to the little boy that he had then rejected everyone, choosing not to become emotionally involved with people.

He chose to be in control, and Maggie had threatened that hard-won control, had broken it. Yes, she understood now; his inner fight against her attraction, the conflict of needs, the savage rejection of her love ... 'love is a killing snare ... crippling'. The harsh words sliced back into her mind. Ian had been emotionally crippled. And there was nothing Maggie could do ... or was there? If she could get to him, bring it all out into the open, make him see ...

She glanced up at Pat, who was eyeing her curiously. 'Thanks for the coffee, Pat. I really must go now. Good luck with the bargain-hunting.'

She strode away quickly, blundering against a couple of chairs in her haste. The shopping crowds jostled her, but she plunged through them, possessed by one idea only, to get to Ian. It was almost three weeks since that disastrous visit to Ian, and now that she saw a glimmer of hope, nothing was going to stop her from seeing him today.

After a long, frustrating wait in the taxi queue at Hyde Park, Maggie was finally on her way. She forced herself to relax during the short trip to Woolhara. Her mind drifted over their turbulent relationship, piecing together the odd reactions he had shown, the revealing words which had made no sense at the time. She would have to keep her emotions under tight restraint if she was to persuade him to talk. He would not welcome her visit nor any personal conversation. But Maggie was very determined, and she was not a person to give up easily. Bert called her a steamroller and she would act like one if necessary.

The taxi pulled up outside the old Woolhara mansion. Maggie paid the driver and stepped out eagerly. It was a beautiful morning. The roses in the garden were in full bloom. She noticed nothing. She ran up the steps, pushed open the front door, strode into the wide hallway and pressed Ian's doorbell.

He did not answer the first summons. She pressed again and again, frustration mounting in her at the continued silence to her call. With disappointment weighing heavily on her heart, she finally turned away.

'Hello, Maggie.' Ian was at the front door, a supermarket bag propped on one arm. His eyes made a cool appraisal of her as she stood dumbfounded. 'I saw you arrive as I was walking down the street.'

'Yes, I . . . I wanted to talk to you,' she forced out nervously. Surprise had robbed her of her earlier confidence.

He nodded, apparently unmoved by her uninvited presence. He fished out a key-ring from the pocket of his casual slacks, found the key he wanted, then looked up with a wry little smile. 'I'm glad you called. I wanted to talk to you away from the work situation.'

She stepped back, digesting that startling information as he inserted the key and opened his door. He waved her in and Maggie walked past him, relieved that it had been so easy, yet conscious of a creeping unease. His manner was too natural, uncaring . . . indifferent? Surely not. He had been forewarned of her visit, she reminded herself sternly.

'I like this room. You must enjoy living here,' she remarked in a light conversational tone.

'Yes. Actually I own the whole house. A pity it's been divided into apartments, but it suits me to keep it that way for the present. There's a solid, lasting quality about these old residences. Craftsmanship in the building that you don't get any more. Will you excuse me for a minute? I'll just unload this bag in the kitchen. Make yourself comfortable,' he added politely.

'Thank you.'

She sat down in an armchair, but her unease grew. Ian's manner was . . . controlled. She breathed a sigh of relief as her confusion cleared. Her gaze wandered around the room, noting its old-fashioned fittings, the antiques which were placed here and there. Solid and lasting. Those qualities would appeal to a man who lacked emotional security.

'Can I offer you a drink? Coffee or . . .'

She shook her head. 'I've just had one . . . with Pat Hollis.'

There was only the merest flicker of something in his eyes, too elusive to define. Then he was raising one eyebrow sardonically. 'Oh? Have you two become friends?'

'It was an accidental meeting. One that neither of us particularly wanted. But . . . it was interesting,' she said with slow deliberation, watching him intently.

Ian shrugged and strolled over to the sofa across from her. He dropped on to it and stretched out his legs, crossing them at the ankles in a pose of complete relaxation. His head was tilted back on the cushions and he observed her through narrowed eyes. He was making it very difficult for Maggie to read his expression.

'I doubt that Pat has the insight to tell you anything interesting, Maggie. About me, that is. Which is why I presume you want to talk to me. However, since you're here, I'd like to apologise for my somewhat emotional outburst the last time you visited me. I very much regret my words and manner to you. It was . . . unkind, to say the least. I assure you that our working relationship will be conducted along more civilised lines.'

'Because that's what you choose to do, isn't it?' she said with a touch of irony. He was in control now, well and truly. The wall of defence he had built around himself was solid, all cracks sealed up, not even the smallest chink showing.

'I can see no point in unnecessary tension,' he replied blandly.

'No, of course not,' she agreed, picking up his

civilised play. 'That's why I think a bit of honest speaking between us might clear the air.'

'I'm not aware that I've been anything but . . . brutally honest with you, Maggie,' he said with a hint of apology.

'You said, quite vehemently, that you'd take Pat back if she'd have you.'

He took it straight on the chin without blinking an eye. 'True. It was said in the heat of the moment. Upon more mature consideration I realised the relationship wouldn't work any more. Pat was neurotically jealous of you. Even as she suggested a reconciliation she spoke continually of you. A marriage riddled with suspicion is not my idea of contentment.'

He put it so reasonably. Much as Maggie would have liked to punch holes in his statement, it did actually fit Pat's recital of the facts. Pat would have interpreted the whole scene from her personal slant, needing to justify Ian's rejection of her offer. Maggie sighed as desolation crept up on her again. One line of attack had been erased. She now had to attempt the other, more tenuous one.

'You didn't tell me you were a deserted child.'

'Why should I? I can't recall your offering any background information either,' he retorted dryly.

'My background didn't affect our relationship. What is it you have against love, Ian? Can't you trust anyone? Is it because your mother deserted you?' she pressed anxiously.

He sighed and pulled an impatient grimace. 'Maggie, I don't need psychoanalysis. I know exactly what I want and why I want it. If Pat has been telling you some sob-story about my childhood, then forget it. I'm not a child any more, and I think most people would view me as a reasonably successful adult.'

He hitched himself forward, elbows resting on his knees, a slight frown of concern on his face. 'Don't hang on, Maggie. It's over. The only involvement I want with you is strictly impersonal. Colleagues at work, that's all. I'm sorry, but you have to let it go. For your own good.'

An apology was the last thing she wanted from him. Inwardly she squirmed under his soft gaze. It reinforced his words, spelling out in capital letters that for him it was over. Her last hope was in its death throes, but it voiced one more appeal.

'I won't hang on, Ian. This is the last time I'll come to you. It's difficult to accept what you're saying, but I'll accept it if you'll just humour me by answering a few questions.'

He bent his head and contemplated the carpet for a few moments, then nodded. 'All right, if it'll make you feel better.'

Maggie bit back the harsh laugh that rose to her lips. Only Ian's surrender would make her feel better. 'I want to know about your mother, why she deserted you,' she said insistently.

'Oh, really, Maggie! Sigmund Freud stuff?' he retorted with an edge of sarcasm. 'I didn't even know my mother, and she didn't desert me. Apparently she had a drug problem and I was a neglected infant. The welfare officers took me away from her. I was about two years of age, barely out of nappies. I don't remember her, never saw her after that, and she died of a drug overdose when I was ten. I was quite content with my life in the orphanage. The authorities were very good to me, and I gave them no trouble. End of story.'

'But you were fostered out, weren't you? Until you were eight or nine?'

It was an uncertain shot, but it hit him and he was not ready for it. The sardonic smile was wiped from his face. His eyes seemed to retreat into darkness, becoming opaque, impenetrable.

'Yes.' He clipped out the word, then adjusted his speech to a more moderate tone. 'It's the usual practice with young children. They're easier to place with families. I was in the care of an English couple who had settled out here. They were childless.'

'And they treated you as their son?' Maggie prompted softly.

His mouth took on a slight twist. 'You could say that.'

'Why did they take you back to the orphanage?'

He made a sharp gesture of irritation and stood up. 'Why do people do anything?' he snapped, then strolled over to one of the windows. He thrust his hands into his pockets as if they irritated him too. 'They had to go back to England. Paul was offered a big promotion. He was sales manager at their branch out here in Australia, but the plum job was in London and it was his for the taking if he went back.'

'Why didn't they take you with them?'

He threw her a look of derision. 'You can't take a fostered child out of the country. That's the law, Maggie. And my mother never did sign adoption papers. They had no choice but to leave me here.'

There had been a choice. They could have turned down the job and stayed here with Ian, if they had loved him enough. Maggie was appalled by their choice, leaving him behind like a toy they had suddenly grown tired of.

'Did they keep in touch? Write to you?'

'No. I imagine they were advised to make a clean break.' He turned and swept her with a cold gaze. 'And I think clean breaks are a good idea, don't you?'

'You should know, Ian,' she said sadly.

'Well, Maggie? Have all these pointless little details made you feel better? Have I done enough humouring?'

He was oh, so hard and relentless. Maggie sighed. She had been fooling herself to think that a man who had conditioned himself to be totally self-sufficient, would suddenly fold up under the pressure of a couple of questions, however painful he found them. He was moving purposefully towards the door. She stood up. Her only chance now was to jolt him out of his set thought patterns.

He held the door open. She walked over and paused beside him. His expression was as unyielding as stone. She took a deep breath and spoke with all the emotion in her heart.

'You say it's over for you, Ian, but it's not for me. I hope you remember the pain and the bewilderment and the bereftness you felt when your foster-parents made their clean break. That's what I feel now. The only difference is that you have no reason at all for turning your back on the love we could have shared. You simply chose to, deliberately, cruelly, and callously. I don't know how you can live with that.'

She paused, but he did not answer her. The tanned skin had paled to sallow and shock registered in every taut line of his face. A savage little triumph burst across Maggie's brain. She had jolted him all right.

Then his lips moved stiffly, as if by an effort of will. 'No.' It was only an explosion of breath, barely a croak. He swallowed and his eyes were stricken with guilt. 'I'm not like them . . . I didn't mean to . . .'

She ignored the agonised protest, as relentless in her purpose as he had been in his. 'It would have been kinder if you'd never looked my way, never spoken to me, never made love to me. Just as it would have been kinder if that English couple had never taken you into their home. You let me taste your love and then you took it away. You chose to shut me out. But I won't let you ignore my grief, Ian. I won't speak of it again, but every time you see me at work, you'll know the torment of loneliness you've condemned me to.'

She left him then, her words hanging over him like a mediaeval curse. His control had been shaken, but it would take time for her words to corrode the defensive wall he had built against her. There was nothing more she could do but wait. And hope.

# CHAPTER NINE

EACH day dragged into the next with no word, no sign of softening from Ian. Maggie worked with concentrated purpose, knowing the account she was handling would eventually force Ian to meet her, if only when she demonstrated her ideas. One of the leading insurance companies had contracted for an extensive advertising campaign to ensure public interest in a new all-inclusive policy. As head of the agency, Ian Drake would have to be at the meeting with the company men. Then she would see how impersonal he managed to be with her.

She drove herself hard, trying to stave off depression. Bert Oliver muttered about steam-rollers and minds like steel traps, but Maggie's mood was too intense to respond to humour. Each day stretched her nerves a little further. There seemed almost a conspiracy in the office to keep thrusting Ian Drake's name at her. Rhonda was the innocent cause of constant irritation. She burst in on Maggie one day, her face gleeful with gossip.

'Guess what! Linda reckons that Ian Drake has broken his engagement. What do you think of that?'

Maggie shrugged, keeping her expression carefully neutral. 'I'd say that's his business.'

'Oh, you're hopeless to gossip to,' Rhonda chided her. 'I think it's absolutely fascinating.

Linda says there haven't been any calls to and fro
and he cancelled a regular order at the florist.
Conclusive, wouldn't you think?' she asked
eagerly.

'Mmm,' Maggie replied noncommittally.

'I wonder why. I thought she was very pretty.'

Rhonda continued speculating for days afterwards, continually dragging Ian's name up.
Maggie's lack of interest did not deter her one
iota. In sheer self-defence Maggie took to going
out for her lunch-hour.

Then there was Peter Cameron to contend
with. He was even more obnoxious since he
assumed that Maggie was more available to his
attentions now that she was unattached to Dan.
When she was at last able to inform him that he
could set up a meeting with the insurance
company, he gave her his customary leer.

'All shaped up, are you?'

'Make it Friday if you can,' she answered
tersely.

'Uh-huh. What are you doing with yourself
these days?'

'Working.'

She turned to leave his office, but he smoothly
barred her way. 'You should relax more, Maggie.
What you need . . .'

'Give it a rest, Peter. I'm not in the mood.'

'You never are,' he snapped, the suave façade
cracking. 'Who do you keep it for? I suppose
you've got your eye on the boss-man now that
he's off the hook. I bet you wouldn't mind
slipping into bed with him.'

Maggie paled and then took a firm grip on
herself. 'Why don't you suggest that to Mr

Drake, Peter? Tell him to give me a call. Who knows? He might be able to interest me. But not you. Not in a million years. So just keep your grubby little mind to yourself.' She side-stepped past him and added silkily, 'Don't forget that meeting, will you? That's your job.'

'You really are a first-class bitch,' he sneered.

'Yes, I like to be first-class at everything,' Maggie retorted acidly, and left him standing.

The meeting was set for Friday morning and Maggie spent all Thursday with Bert Oliver, revising the whole plan of the campaign. By late afternoon she was satisfied that it would be well received.

'Well, we're ready,' she stated wearily.

'Thank God! If there is one,' Bert added irreverently. 'I don't know what's driving you on this one, Maggie, but if I didn't know better, I'd think you were worried that they're not going to like your ideas. But that is plain ridiculous! Those Company men will be hanging accolades all over you tomorrow.'

She gave him an apologetic smile. 'Have I been too awful?'

'Mmm,' he hummed consideringly, and waggled his eyebrows at her. 'I think you owe me a drink or two. Let's go down to the local pub and indulge ourselves.' He leaned forward and waved a disapproving finger at her. 'You need to unwind from being a clockwork doll and it's about time you patted me on my head and said lovely work, Bert. I might be a good and faithful servant, but dammit all, Maggie, I'm not a clockwork dog and I like a bit of appreciation. You've been absolute murder this week.'

She sighed. 'I guess I have been a bit of a pig. I'm sorry, Bert.'

'Did I say pig? You, a pig? My dear girl, I would never dream of going to a pub with a pig. A bitch, yes. I do love bitchy people. They're the spice of life. We shall go and guzzle grog and be gorgeously bitchy about everyone on the staff. I've been saving up some brilliantly cutting comments all week because you weren't in the mood to listen.'

Maggie smiled. Bert was amusing, but right now she could not handle light chit-chat, not with tomorrow getting closer by the minute. 'Do you mind if we take a raincheck on those drinks, Bert? Next week, I promise.'

He pulled a grumpy face, but then turned serious, the wicked twinkle in his eyes fading abruptly. 'What's eating you, Maggie? Having regrets about the break-up with Dan?'

'No.' She gave him a rueful smile and an evasive answer. 'Probably New Year's blues. I'm one year older and going nowhere fast.'

He gave a sympathetic shrug. 'Well, I'm glad you ditched Dan.'

She arched an eyebrow at him and began sorting their work-sheets into the correct order.

'Definitely too good-looking—that was his trouble,' Bert declared knowingly. 'Greek gods are very arrogant, expect everyone to bow to their will. And you're not the bending type, Maggie. You need a man who'll appreciate your worth. Someone like . . . oh, say Ian Drake, for instance.'

Her hands momentarily faltered in her task and her heart skipped a beat. She darted a glance at Bert, hoping that he had not noticed. He was leaning back against his drawing board, elbows hooked on its edge and hands dangling loosely. He had a whimsical smile on his face, but his eyes were observing her keenly. She kept on sorting papers.

'And just what makes you think Ian Drake would appreciate my so-called worth?' she demanded sceptically.

He did not answer directly but chose each word with provocative bite. 'You know, Maggie, coincidences can be extraordinarily curious. Take you and Drake. Both your engagements broke up after our Christmas party. And I don't suppose you've noticed, but while you've had your nose to the grindstone, he's been cracking the whip hard around the office. Short of temper too. No laughs with him. No laughs with you either. Very uptight, both of you.'

She flicked him a derisive look. 'As you say, I haven't noticed.'

'No. But I noticed, Maggie,' he said with insidious softness.

'Well, good for you,' she tossed at him, and quickly tidied the sheaf of papers. Bert was too damned perceptive!

'That really was some Christmas party! I had a hell of a hangover the next day—can't even remember how I got home. I do remember feeling quite sulky that Ian Drake didn't give me a lift. Positive prejudice, I thought. Well, I mean, I know I'm not a gorgeous female, and he didn't dance with me, nor look at me as if he could hardly tear his eyes away, but . . .'

'All right!' she snapped, knowing that it was useless to pretend with him. Her eyes lifted in appeal and she could not disguise the pain his remarks had stirred. 'Just leave it alone, Bert. Please!'

The brown eyes softened with compassion. He nodded and sat in brooding silence as Maggie put the bundle of papers in her folder and stood up. She directed a wry look at him.

'One of these days, Bert, I'm going to hang a patch on that artist's eye of yours. I'll see you in the morning.'

He held up a finger. 'One question, Maggie. He's free. Why don't you take the initiative instead of waiting?'

Her mouth twisted with irony. 'I did. I gambled and I lost. I'll know how far I lost when I see him tomorrow.'

'Hence the tension,' he nodded. He drew in a long breath and declaimed in a slow, precise voice, 'Some men are bloody stupid, not to mention blind, insensitive and just plain bloody-minded.'

Maggie had to smile. Bert never swore. He always said it showed a poor command of the English language. 'I would have to agree,' she said dryly.

'Naturally. Am I ever wrong?' Bert mocked, recovering his usual manner.

'Not so I've noticed.'

'Admirable woman!' He sighed and gave her an encouraging smile. 'Chin up, Maggie. Tomorrow is another day, and for my money, you're a winner. He just doesn't know he's lost yet.'

'I hope you're right about that, my friend,' she tossed at him as she walked away.

She desperately hoped Bert was right. Oddly

enough she did not mind having revealed her feelings to him. He had guessed anyway, and Bert would respect her confidence. Underneath the outrageous veneer he affected, Bert was a very sensitive person with his own special brand of integrity. Her secret was safe with him.

Maggie locked the account folder away in her desk and left the office. The bus stop was thronged with people. When the bus arrived all the seats were already taken and she had to stand in the aisle with passengers crowding in on either side of her. She was not aware of any discomfort as she swayed with the movement of other standing passengers. She was thinking of tomorrow. So much hung on how Ian reacted to her tomorrow.

Suddenly the bus lurched and Maggie was pushed against the backrest of a seat as the people standing behind her lost balance and staggered. She righted herself, rubbing her stomach gingerly. It was almost three weeks past her monthly cycle and she could no longer pretend it was simply late. She had been in such emotional turmoil that she had not noticed at first. Then she had thought up excuses, anything which might be a natural explanation, except the one most natural explanation of all, but each passing day had made her fear more certain. She was desperate now for a favourable sign from Ian, any encouragement at all so that she could reach out to him and not be rebuffed.

The bus pulled up at her stop and she pushed her way through the crush of passengers and alighted. The long hours of evening stretched ahead of her, but there was much to do.

Tomorrow she wanted to look beautiful and no detail of her appearance was to be overlooked. She needed every confidence boost, because fear was gnawing at her, making her nervous and uncertain, uncertain of everything.

Despite a pressing need to do so, Maggie did not sleep well that night. The next morning there was a tired drag to the skin around her eyes. The white blouse she had prepared made her face look even paler. She quickly swapped it for a dusky pink one which looked equally well with her black gaberdine suit. She added blusher to her make-up, hoping to give her face the semblance of a healthy glow. The image which finally looked back at her from the mirror seemed to be perfectly groomed.

Bert was fulsome in his compliments when she arrived at the office. Maggie could only manage a thin smile in response. Her stomach was churning. It had been impossible to force down any breakfast. She felt sick with nervous tension. She flipped through her notes as they waited in the Display Room for the clients to arrive, but her eyes read nothing.

'Loosen up, Maggie,' Bert advised softly. 'You're as tight as a drum.'

'I'll be all right,' she snapped at him irritably.

There was a murmur of voices outside the room and Maggie looked up expectantly. Her heart stopped for a moment as Ian ushered two men into the room. A great welling of love for him swept up her body and shone out of her eyes. But he did not look at her. Even when he performed the introductions his gaze skated over her, not quite meeting her eyes. His face was an impassive mask, his voice smooth, his manner professionally courteous as he gave most of his attention to the Company men.

Maggie grew cold. Her limbs felt stiff. She willed Ian to look at her, really look at her, but he ushered the clients into a row of chairs and sat with them. Not even when he invited her to begin the demonstration did he give her more than a cursory glance. For one frozen moment Maggie did not react. A hand touched her shoulder.

'Shall I begin rolling film now?'

It was Bert to the rescue, gently nudging her to perform. She nodded and plastered a bright smile on her face. Pride demanded that her work be demonstrated to the best of her ability. At first her voice sounded brittle, but it gradually achieved a confident tone. Each phase of the advertising campaign was dealt with competently and Maggie's assurance grew as she felt the approval of the clients. At last it was over and they expressed delighted satisfaction with her concept. Maggie smiled and nodded like an automaton.

Impersonal. The word was echoing hollowly through her brain. There was a detached air about Ian which was totally impersonal. He stood back, saying nothing, letting the clients do all the talking.

'Well, Drake, as long as you have this little lady working for you we won't be looking to any other agency to handle our business,' one of the men declared.

A faint smile curved Ian's lips. 'Miss Tarrington can always be counted on to give satisfaction.'

A little gasp escaped Maggie's lips and her smile stiffened as pain darkened her eyes. Ian's gaze lifted sharply. There was an unguarded flicker of intense emotion, but it was gone in an instant.

'There are few advertising people with her spark of brilliance,' he added quickly.

'Indeed! I hope you recompense her handsomely for her work. Thank you again, Miss Tarrington.'

Maggie accepted the handshake with a veneer of polite pleasure while her mind whirled with tortured thoughts. Satisfaction. Had one night with her satisfied his need? There had been guilt in his eyes. She had made him feel guilty, but he had not changed his mind. He simply could not bear to look at her. She watched him steer the executives out of the room. He was walking away from her and nothing had been resolved. Nothing. She was left alone with Bert. Her body felt as if it was sagging under the weight of her despair.

'Maggie?'

Bert's voice was concerned. She lifted her head and looked at him blankly. Her hand moved instinctively to hold her forehead as the blood drained from her face.

'Bert, I . . .'

Giddiness made her sway. She clutched the back of a chair, but it rocked and overbalanced with her as sickening, dark circles drew her down a black well. She battled her way upwards through wavering layers of consciousness, Bert's voice penetrating the fog in her mind.

'. . . keeled over. She's been very strained all week, working up to this meeting.'

'I can't stay. I'll send Jane Carfield in. Look after her.'

It was Ian's voice and Maggie tried to make her tongue work. She wanted to cry, 'No, stay.' Her eyelids fluttered open, but he was already gone and there was only Bert's worried face looking down at her.

'Maggie? Are you all right?'

'Yes. Just faint,' she mumbled, struggling to get up.

Bert helped her to a chair and insisted she bend over to get her blood circulating properly again. Jane Carfield came in, briskly made her own diagnosis and departed to get a glass of water. Bert fussed around until the secretary returned and held a glass to Maggie's lips.

'Come on now, drink up,' she ordered in her no-nonsense voice. 'You'll feel better in a moment.'

Maggie obeyed, too uncaring to make any protest. Jane Carfield stood back and examined her as she finished drinking.

'You'll be all right. Just sit for a few minutes. I'll go and call a taxi. Mr Oliver, you're to take Miss Tarrington home and get a doctor to her if she needs one.'

'No need,' Maggie whispered.

'Mr Drake's orders, Miss Tarrington. You are to go home and Mr Oliver is to see that you're all right.' Jane Carfield looked down her long nose as if she considered the orders quite unnecessary, but orders were orders and they were to be obeyed implicitly.

'If you say so,' Maggie gave in. She really felt too weak and upset to make a determined protest anyway.

Bert took his responsibility seriously, insisting that she take his arm and handing her into the taxi with elaborate care. She gave him an ironic smile as he settled on to the back seat next to her.

'I feel a real fake. I'm not sick, you know.'

'You could have fooled me,' Bert replied blandly. 'You looked like death when you fainted.'

'A combination of too little sleep, no breakfast and a liberal dose of tension,' Maggie explained wryly.

'That last item I was aware of,' Bert retorted with a sympathetic look. 'If it's any consolation to you Drake didn't appear quite so indifferent when he returned and found you on the floor. In fact, I'll go so far as to say he lost his cool completely. He cursed like a trooper, and it was himself he was savage with. Sounded as if he felt at fault for your fainting.'

A little hope slithered into her heart. 'Did he say why he came back?' she asked cautiously.

'If he had any other reason but you, it wasn't voiced. He was totally concerned with you. There was strong emotion running riot before he pulled himself under control and went off for prim, old long-nose.'

'You think ...' Maggie stopped and sighed. Bert's words could be read several ways. She wanted Ian's love, not his guilt.

'From long experience at observing the odd quirks of human nature, I would say that you haven't lost yet, Maggie, my girl. He might be resisting you for some obscure reason, but you've got a damned good hold on him, believe me,' said Bert with confidence.

'I hope you're right,' she murmured.

He took her hand and gave it a gentle squeeze. 'Now you know I'm almost infallible. Come to think of it, I would have made a good Pope,' he added with a wicked grin.

She relaxed and grinned back at him. He really was outrageous sometimes.

'That's better, Maggie. Those sad grey eyes need a twinkle in them. You shouldn't let any man get you so far down, you know.'

'I suppose not,' she sighed.

He measured her thoughtfully. 'Maybe it's not only a man. Faints aren't part of a healthy scene. Of course, it's not my business . . .'

'No, it's not. And I think you should give that busy mind of yours a rest, Bert. Any minute now it'll be getting jaded from overwork,' she warned him lightly.

He caught the urgent gleam in her eyes and made a wry grimace. 'Your wish is my command, dear girl. My brain is now in neutral.'

Maggie closed her too-revealing eyes and leaned her head back against the seat cushion. Bert tactfully refrained from making further conversation. When the taxi arrived at her apartment building, Maggie insisted that Bert keep it to take him back to work. He insisted that he see her safely into her apartment as per instructions. She was glad of his supporting arm. Her legs still felt like jelly as she walked up the stairs. They had agreed that the taxi could wait for Bert and once she had unlocked her door and stepped inside her living-room he was content to leave her alone.

Maggie closed the door and shut the outside world out. She walked slowly to her bedroom, took off her good clothes and hung them up in her wardrobe, slipped on a housecoat and flopped on to her bed. Her stomach rumbled with hunger. She felt its flatness. It would not stay flat in the months to come if she was pregnant, she thought despondently. Her faint was another ominous sign. Despite the reasons she had given Bert, Maggie was not prone to fainting. She could not remember ever having fainted in her whole life.

Still unwilling to face up to such thoughts, she switched her mind to Ian. Bert's perception of Ian's reaction to her faint gave her room to hope. The strength of his concern for her could also be measured by his subsequent orders. Work had been completely disregarded. Her welfare had been uppermost in his mind. He had sent her home. Maybe, just maybe, he might call on her this afternoon. Please let him come, Maggie willed fiercely. If only he would come, or even telephone, surely they could talk and reach some understanding.

As if in answer to her mental demand the telephone rang. Maggie's pulse leapt excitedly as she jumped off the bed and raced into her living-room. She fumbled with the receiver in her haste, almost knocking it off the table. Then when she finally lifted it to her ear she felt almost too frightened to speak.

'Hello. Miss Tarrington, are you there?'

It was Jane Carfield's voice.

'Yes, yes, it's me,' Maggie answered almost incoherently, expecting the secretary to switch the line through to Ian.

'Mr Drake asked me to call and check that you were all right. Can I assure him of that?'

Disappointment savaged her into anger. 'Put him on the line and I'll tell him exactly how I feel,' she demanded bitterly.

Jane Carfield made a disapproving noise and her voice took on a haughty note. 'Mr Drake is a very busy man, Miss Tarrington.'

'Then tell him he'll have to find out for himself if he's so damned concerned.'

'Miss Tarrington,' the sniff was clearly audible, 'obviously you are not yourself. It is equally obvious that you have recovered from your earlier weakness. I don't think Mr Drake need be troubled further.'

'Oh no, we mustn't trouble him. He wants to be free of any trouble, doesn't he? He wants ...' The click of disconnection was very distinct and Maggie's voice dropped to a dull whisper, '... to be free of me.'

She slowly lowered the handset, staring down at it with seething resentment. 'You could have at least spoken to me. Wasn't I worth a personal word or two?'

Tears gathered in her eyes as she finally hung up. Impersonal. For all Bert had told her, there seemed no point in hoping. Nothing could have been more impersonal than that call from his secretary. Jane Carfield probably thought she was mad, but Maggie didn't care. The hurt had been too great to hold in. It had spilled over into reckless words, but she knew Jane Carfield would not repeat any of them. Ian would be told she was all right.

The hollowness in the pit of her stomach had little to do with hunger, but it reminded Maggie that she had not eaten. She wandered listlessly into the kitchen and looked in the refrigerator. She had not shopped for the weekend and there was nothing to tempt her appetite. Suddenly she did not want to stay in her apartment another minute. Everything oppressed her. Without hesitation she strode into her bedroom, quickly donned jeans and shirt, grabbed her purse and a shopping bag and hurried out.

She would not think about Ian, she decided determinedly. She would pretend this was a holiday. After all, Bert was right. She shouldn't allow any man, or woman, to affect her life so drastically. The Paddington shopping centre had a great deal to offer in the way of distraction with all its arts and crafts and speciality shops.

Maggie treated herself to a light meal at one of the many little restaurants and then strolled around in a desultory fashion, lingering here and there to window-shop. As well as her usual groceries she bought herself some luxury foods, smoked salmon, some chicken liver pâté, a few French pastries and half bottle of really good claret. Not exactly the fare for a sick employee, she thought wryly, but definitely the provisions for pampering, and there was no one else to pamper her.

She passed a pharmacy and then halted. With a heavy sense of fatalism she backtracked and walked determinedly down the shop to the dispensary section. There was no point in hiding her head in the sand. It was time she knew the worst, she reasoned as she bought a pregnancy test kit. Carrying the parcel as if it was dynamite, she returned to her apartment.

That night she steadily ate through the rather odd assortment of delicacies, washing them down with the wine. Going to sleep was no problem, but it was not a restful night. Weird dreams floated across her subconscious, not completely wakening her but not allowing her the peace she needed.

In the morning she followed the instructions on the pregnancy kit. She read the *Sydney Morning Herald* from almost cover to cover as she waited through the two hours required before a result could be ascertained. Politics, world news, letters to the editor, book reviews, sports reports; she read them all, determined not to look at the test until the correct time. The two hours crawled by. Then she looked. The test was positive.

There was not the slightest doubt about her pregnancy any more. The test was undeniably positive. Maggie poured the tell-tale evidence down the drain and walked stiffly out of the bathroom, closing the door behind her with slow deliberation. For a while she stood quite still, the inescapable knowledge pressing down on her. She was pregnant with Ian Drake's child, and Ian did not want to know her.

# CHAPTER TEN

FORCING herself to be calm, Maggie walked into the kitchen and made herself a pot of tea. They give people a cup of tea for shock, she thought vaguely. She told herself that she shouldn't be feeling shock, because she had already known, had known for days, weeks. It was stupid of her to feel shocked. She had to start thinking of what to do.

If only Ian had shown any softness towards her yesterday she would have known what to do, but to have asked Jane Carfield to telephone her was certain proof that he wanted no part of her. Throwing the past in his face had done no good at all. It had actually driven him further away. Her last-ditch effort to make him reconsider had backfired disastrously.

She could not go to him now. He did not want her hanging on, and to hang a child around his neck would make him resent her even more than he did already. She wanted his love, and if he could not give her that, she wanted nothing from him at all. But it is his child, her heart cried despairingly, and I love him so much.

The doorbell rang, jangling her out of her shocked daze. She frowned, wondering who would be calling on her at eleven o'clock on a Saturday morning. She had not had a visitor for weeks, not since Ian. Ian. The name burst across her mind. It had to be Ian. She jumped off the kitchen stool and almost ran to the door, relief pumping through her veins. Her hand could not operate the lock fast enough. At last she flung the door open, her face aglow with anticipation.

'Hello, Maggie. Long time, no see!'

She stared up at Dan's handsome face and the light died out of her eyes. 'Hello, Dan. What are you doing here?' she asked, a tired resignation in her voice.

'How about asking me in? It was a long trip,' he added persuasively.

She stood back and waved him in, too dispirited to argue. 'I was just having a cup of tea. Would you like one?'

'I wouldn't mind. Thanks, Maggie.'

He followed her into the kitchen and propped himself on the stool while she reached down a cup and saucer and poured out the tea.

'You shouldn't have come, Dan. You're wasting your time,' she told him flatly.

'Maybe. Maybe not.' He accepted the cup and eyed her speculatively. 'Whom were you expecting when you opened the door?'

'I wasn't expecting anyone,' she sighed, and leaned back against the sink, her arms folded, her chin lifted at a stubborn angle. 'You might as well accept it, Dan. It's over between us. There's no point in trying again.'

He raised one eyebrow as if sceptical of her statement. 'Maggie, it's six weeks today since you broke our engagement and you don't look as if those six weeks on your own have made you happy. In fact, you look downright miserable, so why don't you let me take you out to lunch? Just friends—no pressure, no arguing. We'll even talk about the weather if you like, but let's share each other's company.'

She shook her head. 'It's no use,' Dan.'

'I've come a long way just to turn around and go back again. Lunch, that's all I'm asking. Be generous, Maggie.'

'I can't.'

'Not even an hour or two? What harm is there in that? You used to enjoy talking to me,' he pressed, his tone light and pleasant, his smile full of persuasive charm.

Maggie looked at him wearily. It had been a mistake to let him in. They had nothing to talk about any more and today of all days was not the time for a superficial chat. She could barely find the will to remain polite. 'Please drink your tea and go, Dan. It's pointless even to talk.'

Anger flashed into his eyes but was quickly erased, an ingratiating smile taking its place. He slid off the stool, swaying a little as he walked towards her. 'Don't be so hard, Maggie. We've had a lot of good times together.' He lifted his hands and dropped them heavily on her shoulders. 'We can have good times again.'

She could smell whisky on his breath now that he was so close. His hands kneaded the soft flesh around her shoulders and her skin suddenly crawled, rejecting the purpose in his touch. 'Take your hands off me, Dan,' she said tightly. 'You can't change my mind.'

'Can't I?'

His tone lost its pleasantness and the words were a rumbling threat. Maggie stiffened as she recognised the hot desire in his eyes, but before she could take evasive action he had pressed her into a close embrace. She pushed at him ineffectually.

'This won't prove anything. Let me go!' she insisted angrily.

'You're mine,' he growled, breathing whisky fumes over her as he bent his head purposefully.

'I'm not yours,' she cried, recoiling from the mouth which was greedily poised to take hers. 'Stop it, Dan! This is stupid. You've been drinking and you're acting unreasonably.'

He ignored her words. His eyes seemed to glaze as he muttered, 'I'll make you mine.'

His arms tightened around her. Maggie tried to break free. She jerked her head away from his questing mouth. Strong fingers thrust through her hair, gripping the nape of her neck and forcing her chin around. Hot lips closed over hers, grinding them against her teeth when she refused to surrender. His thighs trapped her body against the sink and he thrust at her with blatant sexuality. Despite her struggles his free hand tore at her shirt. Buttons gave and he dragged the material down over one shoulder. He released her mouth and stared downwards as his hand cupped her bared breast, lifting, squeezing, kneading the rounded flesh in gloating possession. His breath was coming in harsh gasps, and Maggie panicked.

'No!' she choked out. Then in an explosion of fear and defiance she threw at him the two words which could damn her in his eyes. 'I'm pregnant!'

He looked up dazedly. 'What? What did you say?' he demanded in harsh disbelief.

'I said I'm pregnant,' she flung at him recklessly, finding a strange satisfaction in the words now that they had been spoken. 'I'm pregnant. That's what I said, and it's true, so now you know that I'm not yours and never will be, so let me go.'

'You bitch!'

The hard slap had her reeling sideways and she looked back in stunned horror at the snarling contempt on his face.

'All those months of holding me off and you jump straight into bed with the first guy who comes along!'

Again his hand cracked across her face, rocking her against the pantry wall. She slid down to the floor, holding up her arms to ward off any more blows.

'Or were you two-timing me? Sleeping with someone else while playing Goody Two-Shoes with me? Did the chickens come home to roost at an inconvenient time? A bit awkward to marry me with a bastard in your belly! You tramp!' he spat at her.

Maggie flinched, terrified that he meant to kick her. Violence distorted the lines of his face and he was indeed a total stranger to her.

'You can stop cowering,' he sneered. 'I wouldn't dirty my hands on you any more. I hope you rot in hell!'

He spun on his heel and stormed out of her apartment, slamming the door shut behind him. Maggie was trembling all over. Her head was still ringing from his blows and her face hurt. She felt it tentatively. Her lip was cut. Blood showed on her finger. She stared at it, trying to get her mind back into working order.

The violence from Dan had been so unexpected, exploding upon her with devastating force. But she had pressed the trigger. It had been the height of stupidity, a cruel, unnecessary provocation to hurl her pregnancy in his face. It had been a stinging blow to his pride, his manhood. Dan had not deserved that. She could hardly blame him for lashing out at her, but it still stunned her that he had been so vicious about it.

Slowly she dragged herself up and staggered into the bathroom. A red puffiness around one eye promised an ugly bruise. She rinsed away the blood from her lip and examined the wound gingerly. The cut was not deep and would heal soon enough, but already the lip was swollen and spongy. Feeling thoroughly shaken, Maggie decided the only thing to do was lie down for a while. She was heading for her bed when the telephone rang.

Her nerves jumped in protest. She stared at the telephone resentfully, not at all inclined to speak to anyone. Only the persistent little hope that it might be Ian forced her to pick up the receiver.

'Maggie?'

'Yes, Mum.' Maggie's voice was a trembling mumble. A choking wave of emotion was sweeping through her, building momentum as the familiar voice at the other end of the line spoke with loving concern.

'. . . understand why you can't come home, dear. It's been almost a month since I've seen you, and . . .'

Suddenly Maggie felt as if she was drowning, sinking under the weight of too many burdens, and there was only her mother to turn to for help. 'Mum . . .' It was a croak of need, bursting from her throat as tears gushed into her eyes. 'Mum, please come . . . I need you—I need you here. I can't come home. Please, Mum!' The words were punctuated by gasping sobs and the tears would not stop.

'Maggie dear, you sound so distraught! What's wrong?'

'I can't . . . please come!'

'I'll be on the first train I can catch,' her mother said with firm decision. 'Now you just put yourself to bed, Maggie, and I'll be right in to look after you. Is there anything you need? Anything I can bring you?'

'No . . . just yourself.'

'Don't you worry, dear. I'm coming.'

Maggie fumbled the receiver down and blundered into the bedroom, crawling on to the bed and curling into a ball. She rocked herself in mindless despair, weeping tears of utter hopelessness into the pillow. Everything was so wrong. Ian did not want her. Dan despised her. She was going to have a baby and she didn't know what to do. But her mother was coming. Her mother would help sort it all out. Her mother loved her. Sheer mental and physical exhaustion eventually drew her into a sluggish sleep.

The blank fog of merciful nothingness was disturbed by a jabbing noise. Maggie tried to resist it, instinctively shrinking from full consciousness. The noise would not go away. She lay with her eyes closed for a few moments longer. The ache in her face and the spongy fatness of her bottom lip sent painful messages to her brain. The doorbell was ringing. Her mother had arrived.

Maggie scrambled off the bed. A quick glance in the mirror made her wince. An ugly discoloration around one eye and her puffy mouth did absolutely nothing to lighten her rock-bottom spirits. She quickly turned away and hurried to the front door.

Her mother would inevitably be shocked, not only by the disfigured face but by everything which had to be disclosed. There was no escaping the truth, and the sooner it was faced the easier it would be to come to grips with it. With a bleak sense of resignation, Maggie released the lock and swung the door open.

Ian Drake stood there. There was one frozen moment which lasted an agonising length of time. Shock faded, and horror stamped itself on Ian's face. Maggie's heart thumped a piteous protest. She recoiled from him, her hands automatically fluttering up to hide the bruises and swelling.

'Maggie . . .' It was a strangled cry of alarm. He stepped forward, one arm stretching towards her.

In mindless panic she spun away, the fear of another rejection shooting through every nerve, but before she could flee, strong hands caught and halted her.

'For God's sake! What's happened to you?'

She covered her face with her hands as he insistently turned her back to him. 'Don't!' she begged, unable to bear a cold scrutiny of her distress.

'Maggie . . .'

His voice was soft with compassion. Then his arm was around her shoulders, warm and comforting as he drew her over to one of the armchairs and gently settled her into it. There was a touch on her hair, a tender, stroking caress.

'Don't be upset—please!' The tone was anxiously placating. 'I wasn't prepared, that's all. I had to see you. I just wasn't expecting . . . oh hell!'

This last was a sigh of despair. She sensed his move away and started up in agitation, every instinct clawing at her to implore him to stay. He was striding towards the door.

'Ian!'

Her cry of need stopped him. He turned and the torment in her soul was reflected on his face.

'Don't go!' Maggie begged desperately.

'I'm not going. I left the door open.'

He moved the few extra paces required to shut it then turned back. Maggie slumped down into her chair, weak with relief, and tried to collect her disjointed wits into some coherent working order. Ian was here. He had come to see her. What for? The question screamed across her brain, urgent, demanding, burdened with all the despair in her heart. She glanced fearfully at him as he drew the other armchair close to hers. He angled it so that they were almost facing before sitting down. She flinched from his searching gaze, turning her head to one side to minimise his view of her disfigurement.

'How did this happen?'

She glanced at him uncertainly, unable to argue his reaction from the taut, controlled voice. 'It's nothing really. It just looks bad,' she said tentatively. 'I . . . I didn't think it could be you. Not . . . not after yesterday. I thought it was my mother. She said she'd come.'

A pained look crossed his face. He leaned forward, his body tense. 'Maggie, answer me! You look as if . . .'

'I'm all right, it's only my face,' she rushed in, not wanting him sidetracked on to something which was completely unimportant at the moment.

'Only your face!' he exclaimed in exasperation. 'Have you seen a doctor?'

'No. I told you, there's no real harm done—just a cut lip and a black eye. Don't fuss, Ian, you'll only make me feel worse.'

He rubbed at his brow then drew in a deep breath and let it out slowly. 'You've called your mother,' he said, as if he needed to set his mind straight.

'Yes. I . . . I needed someone. I . . . felt . . .'

'Who hit you?'

The question was sharp, insistent, tearing through her shaky defences. She evaded his gaze and sought to evade an answer, but she could not think of anything but the truth. She looked down at her hands. They were trembling, and she squeezed them tightly. 'I don't want to talk about it,' she mumbled.

'Should the police be called?'

Shock jerked her head up. 'No, of course not!'

'Why not?' he continued relentlessly.

Anger simmered in his eyes and she realised that he had to be told. It was the only way to dismiss the subject. 'It was Dan,' she said bluntly.

The air vibrated with tension. Ian's hands clenched into tight fists. Maggie rushed into further explanation, trying to defuse the violence she sensed.

'He came here this morning and . . . and the situation got out of control. I made him angry and he lashed out at me.'

'The bastard!' It was an explosive mutter, full of venom. 'Why, Maggie?' he shot at her.

She sighed and answered in a dull monotone, feeling more miserable by the minute. 'He wanted us to try again, and he didn't want to take no for an answer.'

'Did he . . . did he rape you?'

The harsh words grated on her ears. She shook her head. There was a sharp expulsion of breath from Ian and his hands slowly unclenched.

'But he tried.' The words were coated with contempt.

'Not really.' Her hands fluttered in nervous protest. 'It was my fault. I shouldn't have said what I did. He'd been drinking and . . . and I didn't want him to kiss me, so I said . . . I said I was sleeping with another man. I'd never let Dan make love to me, and he just exploded into violence.'

There was a short silence and again tension grew.

'Was that all you said, Maggie?'

Scorching heat burnt across her cheeks as the words she had spoken to Dan seared themselves on her brain. She could not look at Ian—dared not. There was too much fear and uncertainty in her heart. She pushed herself up and forced her shaky legs to pace away from him. Her arms hugged tightly to the inner pain.

'Why did you come, Ian?' she asked in a desperate little voice.

'I was worried about you,' he replied quietly, and there was a thread of anxiety in his tone.

'Worried!' She made a brittle sound which was half laugh, half sob. 'Of course, you didn't have Jane Carfield on hand today. That was a pity wasn't it? You could have asked her to telephone for you.'

'I needed to see you.'

Maggie's heart gave a great leap and began pounding erratically. She sucked in a deep breath and swung around to face him. 'Why?'

His eyes were filled with dark torment. 'I had to know. I couldn't ignore the possibility. It's been gnawing at me since you fainted yesterday. You were a virgin, and I didn't take precautions that night.'

He paused as if he found the words too difficult to say. Maggie knew what was coming and she wasn't prepared for it. She didn't know how he felt, how he would react, and it was so terribly important to her.

'Are you pregnant?'

She stared at him, too frightened to answer. If he rejected her now . . .

'You are, aren't you?' he insisted.

'Yes,' she whispered.

He groaned and covered his eyes with his hand. Stung by his seemingly negative reaction, Maggie poured out her pain in a deluge of words.

'You don't have to worry, Ian. I don't hold you responsible. I asked for it, didn't I? You warned me . . . one night, Maggie, that's all . . . that's what you said. Only I didn't believe you. But that's not your fault—I wanted you to love me. But I won't hang on, Ian. I didn't tell you, you asked. You didn't have to ask me . . .' Then as there was no response from him, the last tenuous thread on her control broke, and her voice rose to a scream of anguish. 'Oh, go away! Go away! Don't torture me like this. I can't take any more!'

He stood, but instead of moving towards the door he stepped towards her. Through a blur of tears Maggie saw his hands stretch out, but she was beyond any coherent thought now. All the spent emotion of the day had taken its toll. She backed away from him, trembling with the force of her inner turmoil.

'Don't touch me! You don't care. You wouldn't even look at me. You got your secretary to call—you wouldn't even speak to me. Not a word. I don't want anything from you, do you hear? Not your sympathy, not money—nothing! You can go, be free. Don't touch me!'

It was a hoarse, despairing cry. Her hands tried to beat him off, but he quietly and forcefully gathered her in. Strong arms enfolded her, pressing her in to the warmth of his body. Gentle hands soothed away her resistance. Weak and helpless, Maggie laid her head on his shoulder and wept uncontrollably. He rubbed her back in soft comfort and the shuddering sobs gradually degenerated into little hiccups. Ian stroked her hair and the tenderness in his touch slowly seeped through her misery to the inner core of desperate need.

She wanted him to go on holding her for ever. For a little while she indulged herself, silently accepting his soft caress and pretending it was the touch of love. But pretence was no good; it had to be real. She stirred herself reluctantly.

'You can let me go now, Ian. You've done enough nursemaiding. I won't collapse.'

They were brave words, proud words, and he ignored them. His arms tightened around her.

'Maggie . . .' There was an excruciating pause and then, '. . . Oh God! How do I even begin to speak to you?'

It was a groan of despair. She could have told him to say nothing, just to love her, but there had been too many words between them and pride would not let her repeat the folly of loving without commitment. His fingers threaded through her hair and pressed her head back against his shoulder.

'Maggie, will you listen to me?' The plea was rasped out, as if grating over too many emotions for clarity.

'Yes, I'll listen to you,' she muttered dully, anticipating more pain but compelled to hear what he had to say.

He led her back to the armchair she had vacated and saw her comfortably settled. 'Can I get you anything . . . a hot drink?' he asked anxiously.

'No, thank you. I'm sorry about the hysterics. It's been that kind of day.' She sighed and looked up at him guardedly. 'I'm listening, Ian.'

He straightened. The anxiety was still in his eyes, a turbulent mixture of doubt and determination. 'You weren't going to tell me, were you, Maggie?'

'How could I?' she threw at him bitterly. 'You would have called it emotional blackmail. That was your phrase, wasn't it? You said you didn't owe me anything. And you don't.'

He took his chair again, sitting forward with his elbows on his knees. He squeezed his eyelids between finger and thumb, then looked up at her wearily. 'I said a lot of stupid things,' he muttered in self-disgust, 'and every last one of them was motivated by an overdeveloped sense of self-preservation. I was obsessed with . . . my ideas . . . my life . . . my needs.' He bent his head, shaking it as if appalled by his own selfishness. 'I'm . . . mortally ashamed that my attitude has forced you to bear this alone. I . . . I don't know how else to put it. To say I'm sorry is totally inadequate.'

He lifted agonised eyes. 'But I am sorry, Maggie, please believe me. I know it must have been hell for you this last couple of weeks. And yesterday . . . yesterday was unforgivable, in the circumstances.' He bent his head again, raking agitated fingers through his hair. 'I didn't even think of consequences until yesterday. But now . . .' He looked up and his outstretched hands lent emphasis to the desperate appeal in his eyes. 'You must consider the child, Maggie. It's our child. We have to do what's best for it.'

His self-condemnation had stirred her interest and his apology had eased some of the ache in her heart, but those last words scraped painfully over the hope she had begun to nurse. 'I see.' There was the chill of rejection in her voice. 'And just what do you think is best for our child, Ian?'

He winced at the cold tone. His hands lifted and fell in a hopeless little gesture. 'Maggie, no matter how good a wage-earner you are, or how well-intentioned you may be, a single parent is still in a disadvantaged position. It would be so much easier for you, better for the child. You'd have more time, no worries. I could provide so much for both of you . . . if you'll marry me.'

'Marry you!'

It was a stunned gasp. Maggie had prepared herself to reject a financial arrangement but . . . marriage! He was proposing marriage! Then reason whispered that he was intent on the role of father, not husband. Being a husband to her was incidental. Ian was remembering his own insecure, lonely childhood. He would want to give his own child everything, most of all the protection of married parents. His proposal was not a surrender to her but a sacrifice to principle. His child would have the father Ian himself had never had.

The sharp zing of the doorbell dispersed the jumble of feverish thoughts. Maggie threw a defensive look at Ian. 'It must be my mother.'

He frowned and nodded.

She pushed herself to her feet. It was unfortunate that her mother should arrive at this critical moment, but there was nothing Maggie could do but let her in. If Ian was really determined on marriage, his proposal would stand. It seemed a gigantic step away from his former position of non-involvement, and Maggie needed time to consider all the implications. Perhaps her mother's visit might provoke Ian into declaring his feelings more openly. In the turmoil of the moment, Maggie completely forgot her injured face.

# CHAPTER ELEVEN

'THANK goodness! I was beginning to wonder . . .
Oh, Maggie!'

Maggie sighed as her mother's expression
forcefully reminded her of her appearance. 'Come
in, Mum,' she invited quickly, staving off the
imminent barrage of questions. She grabbed hold
of the suitcase near the doorway and steered her
mother inside.

'Oh, dear—your poor face!' Fay Tarrington
wailed, but the wail stopped abruptly when she
caught sight of Ian who was advancing to meet
her.

'Mrs Tarrington,' he nodded, smoothly ex-
tending a hand in greeting. 'I'm Ian Drake.'

'Drake?' she echoed in bewilderment until
realisation dawned. 'Oh yes, Mr Drake. You're
the head of the agency where Maggie works. But
what . . .?' She looked her puzzlement at Maggie.
'Did you have an accident at the office, dear?'

'No. It was this morning, Mum, just before
you called. That's why I was so upset,' Maggie
explained quickly. 'Ian's here as . . . as a friend.'

'Oh!' Fay Tarrington turned measuring eyes
on to the man who was relieving her daughter of
the suitcase. 'I thought you'd want me to stay,
Maggie,' she said questioningly.

'Yes, I do, Mum. Thanks for coming.' Maggie
kissed her on the cheek and gave her an
affectionate hug.

'Do you want this put in the bedroom?' Ian asked matter-of-factly.

'Yes, please.'

The startled look in her mother's eyes warned Maggie that Ian's casual enquiry had sparked off a rapid train of speculative thought. 'Want a cup of tea or coffee, Mum?' she asked in an attempt at distraction.

'I think I could do with one,' her mother answered slowly. 'Coffee, please, dear.'

'Coffee, Ian?'

'Thank you,' he called back, apparently intent on staying and not at all perturbed by her mother's visit.

Maggie headed into the kitchen. Her mother followed, her eyes sharp with questions in a face which was creased with concern.

'Maggie, what's going on?' she hissed. 'And you look dreadful! You should have been coming home at weekends. I've been worrying about you since New Year.'

'I'm sorry, Mum. I didn't mean to worry you, but . . .' She shrugged, helpless to explain everything in a few moments.

'And what's Ian Drake doing here? You've only ever mentioned him as your employer.'

Maggie flicked her mother an anxious look of appeal. 'He's the man I told you about,' she murmured quickly.

Fay Tarrington's eyes rounded in alarm as Ian reappeared.

'Maggie, why don't you sit down with your mother and let me make the coffee?' he offered, making his familiarity with her apartment even more pointed.

Maggie flushed and evaded her mother's questioning gaze. 'No, thanks, I'm fine really. Mum, you go and sit down with Ian. I'll only be a minute.'

'Yes, all right, then,' her mother replied with a suspicious amount of relish. 'Come, Mr Drake. I'd like to have a little chat with you.'

Maggie's heart dropped to the bottom of her stomach. Her mother's tone of voice suggested an uncompromising headmistress about to tackle a recalcitrant boy. She glanced apprehensively at the pair of them, but neither was looking her way. Her mother sat down with a very straight back. Ian settled into the opposite armchair, his gaze fixed unwaveringly on Fay Tarrington.

'I recollect Maggie telling me at Christmas time that you were engaged to be married to some very nice girl,' her mother opened up with an air of taking the bull by the horns.

'I don't intend marrying anyone but your daughter, Mrs Tarrington,' Ian answered with devastating directness.

The electric jug boiled. Frantic not to miss a word and with every nerve stretched in agonised tension, Maggie jerked out the cord and splashed water over the instant coffee.

'Well, Mr Drake ...' came the surprised rejoinder.

'Ian.'

'You've quite taken my breath away!'

'I'm sorry. I thought it best to apprise you of my intentions so you could understand the situation.'

'Well! I don't know you, Mr Drake. And I certainly don't understand the situation.'

'The situation is very simple.'

They both turned at Maggie's terse interjection. She stood in the doorway to the kitchen and threw a look of defiant challenge at Ian before concentrating on her mother.

'You might as well know, Mum. I was going to tell you later anyway. I'm pregnant. Ian only wants to marry me because I'm expecting his child. I'm sorry, but that's how it is.'

Shock gave way to anxiety on Fay Tarrington's face. Her gaze flickered from Maggie to Ian and back again. 'The other girl?' she asked sharply.

'My engagement to Pat was broken a couple of days after Maggie ended hers with Dan Barlow,' Ian stated with cool precision. He had answered her mother, but now his eyes lifted to Maggie and fixed on hers with hard intensity. 'At the time I thought I wanted to stay free, but I've since realised how wrong I was.'

'Are you quite sure of that, Ian?' Maggie snapped. Goaded by his calm, unemotional manner she fiercely attacked his assertion. 'Don't you think it's rather premature to bind yourself to a child who isn't born yet? Who knows? I might have a miscarriage and you can still be free!'

'Maggie!'

The sharp reproof from her mother brought a painful rush of blood to Maggie's cheeks. She turned back to the kitchen, slightly ashamed of her outburst but with no intention of making an apology. She was churning with the memories of too many hurts. Her hands trembled as she loaded the coffee on to a tray. She took it into the living-room and served it, her lips thinned in determined silence. Her mother threw her a worried look as Maggie sat herself at the corner table, but Maggie remaind stubbornly silent. If Ian wanted marriage, he could do the talking!

Fay Tarrington turned a stern gaze to Ian. 'Mr Drake, I've always considered that an unplanned pregnancy was a poor basis for marriage. Your sense of honour does you credit, but if that's the only motive for your proposal . . .'

'It's not my only motive, Mrs Tarrington,' he assured her quietly, 'but it's probably the only one Maggie will believe. My behaviour towards her throughout our relationship is a matter of deep regret to me. Unfortunately I can't change the past. I hope to make amends to her in the future.'

'Presuming there is a future,' Maggie put in curtly. 'Don't presume too much, Ian. I haven't said yes.'

He turned to her, his eyes dark with implacable determination. 'I've hurt you very badly. From any reasonable viewpoint you should reject me, but I'm not talking reason, Maggie. I'm talking need. Right now you might think I'm the last person you need, but two weeks ago you demanded that I remember something. I did. I know exactly what you feel towards me and you have ample justification for feeling the way you do. But now I'm asking you to remember . . .'

He was not unemotional now. He spoke quietly, but each word was delivered with passionate force. 'Remember a night when we shared something special . . . so special it was unique and unforgettable. Despite my blind selfishness and despite your bitter hatred, you can't deny what there is between us, any more

than I can. We need each other. And we'll be
mother and father to the child we made together,
because even if nothing else has been right
between us, that night was. And somehow we'll
make it so again. We have to. We're linked
together now whether we like it or not. It's
inescapable—you know that.'

He paused, drawing in a deep breath before
driving home his final point. 'You might as well
say yes, Maggie, and get it over with. Your
mother's here. We can start discussing wedding
plans.'

'Just like that!' Maggie muttered resentfully,
then raised her voice in bitter accusation. 'You
expect me to accept you, just like that! You
wouldn't even look at me yesterday, nor speak to
me. And today you expect me to marry you!'

Her voice rose higher with pent-up feeling.
'You're damned right, I have every justification
for rejecting your offer. And I have almost
insurmountable reservations about accepting you
as a husband. You do well to invoke the memory
of that night, Ian. It was the only time you ever
gave me any happiness. I'm not so desperate to
provide my baby with a father that I'll marry a
man who doesn't want me!'

'Our baby,' he said insistently. 'I am its father.
And I want you, Maggie. Anything I've said to
the contrary was a lie. I tried to fight you, but I
can't, and I don't want to any more. Say what
you want, and if it's within my power, I'll give it
to you.'

His complete volte-face confused her. 'Does a
child mean so much to you, Ian?' she asked in
bewilderment.

'Your happiness is my first consideration.'

She shook her head in disbelief and scorn edged her voice. 'Since when?'

'Since I realised what a fool I'd been to have squandered your gift of love.'

His tone was one of quiet sincerity and his eyes silently begged for another chance. She wanted to believe him, needed to believe him. She was frightened of the consequences if it was all a ruse to get his own way. She looked for help from her mother, but Fay Tarrington was regarding Ian thoughtfully.

'Mum?'

Her mother looked at her with sympathetic enquiry, but Maggie felt too confused to express the doubts which were bombarding her mind with barbs of indecision. She fluttered her hands helplessly. Fay Tarrington stood and walked over to her. Her hand gave Maggie's shoulder a light squeeze as her eyes softened with a warm reassurance of love.

'Only you know if you can find the necessary forgiveness in your heart, Maggie, but I remember what you told me at Christmas time. He is turning to you now. I can't help you make what must be your decision. I think it best if I take myself off to a movie and leave the two of you alone for a while. All right?'

'Yes, all right. But you'll come back?'

'Of course.' A comforting smile softened her mouth. 'I'm going to cook you dinner and tuck you into bed—that's what mothers are for!'

Maggie covered her mother's hand with her own and attempted a smile in response. 'Thanks, Mum,' she said gratefully.

Fay Tarrington turned to Ian, who had risen to his feet. 'I'm trusting you not to hurt my daughter any more, Mr Drake. I'll reserve my own judgment of you. You'll appreciate that so far you've done little to commend yourself to me.'

'I appreciate it all too well, Mrs Tarrington. Thank you for your forbearance,' he answered gravely.

Ian accompanied her mother to the door and saw her out. Maggie did not move. She felt very unsure of everything and worn out by the conflict of emotions which was still fraying what little strength she had left. With intense weariness she propped her elbow on the table and rested her head on her hand, wishing she did not have to think any more. She watched Ian's approach with dull resignation. He looked slightly unsure of himself too, which made her feel slightly better. She wished he would lose hold of his iron control. She wished he felt as weak and as vulnerable as she did. She wished . . .

'Maggie . . .' His hand reached out and stroked the silky waves of her hair.

She shuddered at the soft caress and looked up at him in helpless appeal, wanting so much from him but unable to ask.

Very gently he lifted her to her feet, his eyes seeming to plead for her compliance. Then slowly, watchful for any sign of resistance, he drew her into a tender embrace. There was no resistance in Maggie. She stood in the circle of his arms, wanting him to answer all her needs but with little faith or hope in any of her wishes. The empty places inside her deflated with a shuddering sigh as warm hands coaxed her closer.

'Maggie . . .' His breath wavered through her hair as he laid his cheek on it. His voice was a husky murmur, vibrating softly through her brain. 'I know it'll be difficult for you to believe. It took me too long to face up to it myself. But I do love you, Maggie, so very much. I need you—more than I ever believed it possible to need another human being. I want the child, that's true. But you are necessary to me. I'm incomplete without you.'

The sweet words were a soothing drug, anaesthetising pain, but sharp needles of reason jabbed in reminders of too many inconsistencies for an avowal of love to be credible. 'Please, Ian. I'm not stupid,' she dragged out wearily. 'You've done very well without me since Christmas.'

'No, Maggie. It's been tearing me apart,' he insisted, and the pain of torment was in his voice. 'I've wanted you all the time. It's been one hellish struggle against running back to you ever since I rejected your love. I thought I didn't want to belong to anyone. All these years I've kept a wall between myself and the emotional inconsistencies of other people. I don't like to feel vulnerable, Maggie, but I can't bear to be alone any more, not having known you. These last two weeks, I thought I'd made you hate me, that I'd hurt you too much and it was too late to reach back. I deserved your hatred, but yesterday . . . yesterday I shrank from seeing it in your eyes. Then you fainted . . .'

His hands ran slowly over her as if in need of reassurance that she was really there. 'Oh, God! How I wanted to gather you up in my arms and take care of you! But I'd given you enough pain and I had to leave you to others. I couldn't believe you'd want me there, upsetting you further. I got Jane Carfield to ring you because I had to know if you were all right. I thought you'd hang up on me. Today . . .' He sighed and drew in a steadying breath. 'Today I couldn't stay away any longer. I was determined to use anything, Maggie—the child, if you were pregnant; your mother, if she favoured marriage. Anything to have you again. I'm a selfish bastard through and through, Maggie, but I swear I'll earn your love again if you'll let me try. Say it's not too late!'

The desperate plea was an echo of her own despair, and as it faded away, so did all the pain, the fear, and the torment. She slid her hand up, over his chest to his heart, savouring the strong beat of it and knowing at last that it beat in unison with hers, a drumming confirmation of love. She sighed in contentment and nestled her head under his chin to feel the warmth of his throat. 'You don't have to earn my love, Ian,' she murmured happily. 'It's yours. It's been waiting for you all along—waiting and yearning for you to accept it.'

She felt the leap of his heart, heard his sharp intake of breath. Then his fingers were threading through her hair, moving urgently to pull her head back so that he could assure himself of the truth in her eyes. He looked down at her with incredulity, wonder, joy, and the most intense relief.

'Maggie, you must have the most giving heart of all. I'll treasure you all my life.'

There was such depth of emotion in his voice that if Maggie had nursed any final doubt, it was banished for ever. Ian loved her! With a smile of exultation he lifted her up, cradling her against his chest as one does a beloved child. He carried her over to an armchair and sat down, settling her comfortably and tenderly on his lap.

'I'll take the greatest care of you, my darling, I promise you.' His lips moved softly over the unbruised half of her face in a worshipful trail of kisses. 'I should have been here this morning to protect you,' he murmured regretfully.

'It doesn't matter. You're here now.' She reached up and caressed his cheek, glorying in the wonderful fact that she could touch him without fear of rebuff. He was hers. They were one with each other and no longer would they ever be parted in spirit.

'We'll get married as soon as possible,' he declared with firm resolution.

'Yes,' she agreed, only too happy to agree with him about anything.

'Do you want a big wedding?'

'Not particularly. I just want you. But I guess we'll have to ask a few people. Mum will insist!'

He made a wry gimace. 'I hope I can win your mother's approval.'

'You will. She only wants to see me happy. And married. And providing her with a grand-child. How can you miss when you're doing all three?'

'I almost did miss,' he replied seriously, the remembrance of pain shadowing his eyes. 'How can you forgive me, Maggie? I was so . . .'

She placed a silencing finger on his lips. 'It's

past, Ian. I don't want to waste another minute with you. We're going to be positive and only share happiness. After all, we control our lives, don't we?' she teased.

He smiled. 'Yes, we do. Two piranhas in a bowl. We're going to make a fierce combination, you and I.'

'Yes. Isn't it marvellous!'

His smile became a grin and their eyes sparkled with the shared knowledge of each other.

'Magic, my beautiful witch,' he declared.

And it was magic, a special magic which pulsed between them, conjured up by the power of love, a love fully acknowledged, given and returned.

## QUICK AND DELICIOUS PÂTÉ

Maggie treats herself to a little luxury when she purchases, among other delicacies, chicken-liver pâté. If you want to treat yourself, but wish to save money at the same time, why not try this recipe for making your own chicken-liver pâté? It's easy, quick and delicious.

What you need:

2 medium onions, coarsely chopped
1/4 lb. butter
10 chicken livers
2 eggs
1/4 tsp. marjoram
1/8 tsp. nutmeg
1/8 tsp. ground cloves
salt and pepper to taste
2 tbsp. dry sherry
parsley
a large frying pan
a blender

What to do:

In frying pan, sauté onions in butter. Add chicken livers and cook until pink. Break eggs into pan and cook until all bits of yolk are done, not runny. Add marjoram, nutmeg, cloves, salt and pepper. Pour contents into blender. Turn on blender, adding sherry gradually, till a purée results. Pour into large bowl and garnish with parsley. Cover and cool for two hours in fridge. Remove one hour before serving. Great with crisp toast or crackers.